SUMMER HIKER

Terry Shepherd

Summer Hike
© Terry Shepherd 2025

ISBN: 978-1-923289-60-4 (Paperback)
Cover Design: Terry Shepherd and Clark & Mackay
Format and Typeset: Terry Shepherd and Clark & Mackay
Published by Terry Shepherd and Clark & Mackay
Proudly printed in Australia by Clark & Mackay

Contents

A DEADLY DRIVE

The sun is setting on yet another scorching summer afternoon. Michael has committed his second murder in three months. As he is driving away from where he left the body, not caring if it is found, his mind drifts into a state of calm. He's thinking of the fishing trip he has been planning for a few weeks.

As a truck driver for a lumber company, Michael does a lot of driving, from multiple drops in the city to the occasional country drive. It's a lonely job, so when the opportunity presents itself, he will gladly pick up a hitchhiker. His latest victim was on her way to the upper coast of New South Wales (NSW), planning a week of sunbaking at Yamba. Michael was on his way to Coffs Harbour with a load of western red cedar when he picked up Angelina at a truck stop just north of Newcastle.

'Another coffee, please, Jacko,' yells Michael to the long-term waiter there. He's a regular at this truck stop, and most people there know him as a charming, fun bloke, a little loud sometimes, but always good for a laugh.

'Hey mister, are you headed north? I'd love a ride if ya have the room,' asks Angelina.

'Sure, love, just gonna finish me coffee and we'll hit the road.'

So, Angelina sits opposite Michael with her innocent grin and tries to strike up an conversation. But before she has the chance, Michael asks her, 'So, how old are ya, love?'

Shyly replies that she is nineteen and is travelling around the country before deciding on any career choice.

'I finished school last year and decided to see our beautiful country before looking for work. The only problem is, I have no idea what kind of work I want to do,' explains Angelina. 'Well, I'm sure once you have seen enough of the country, you'll have it all worked out. Wanna grab any snacks before we head out? Next stop is four hours away,' says Michael.

'Thanks all the same but I have enough in my knapsack to keep me going for a while,' Angelina replies with her cute smile.

'Alrighty then, time to head out,' says Michael as he walks over to the counter to pay his bill.

Another routine truck drive and many hitchhikers picked up along the way – it's like Russian roulette – not even Michael knows when he will turn. Sadly, Angelina never made it, as, for some strange reason, Michael pulled the truck over after driving for nearly three hours. He suggested that Angelina get out and stretch her legs, as the brakes would take a little while to cool down.

'We can't continue driving with the brakes so hot, we'd be screwed if the brakes failed altogether,' explains Michael.

So, naturally she gets out, with a helping hand. The rig is a bit of a climb for a short young lady. Just as she stretches, she is hit in the side of the head with a steel bar kept hidden in the trailer. She is repeatedly beaten until Michael is out of breath. He then falls to the ground, exhausted, and lights up a cigarette to celebrate his achievement. Once he completes this horrid habit – one day, he swears he is going to give them up for good – he carries the body a good distance into the scrub, where it will be very hard to find.

'Must book that deep-sea fishin' trip with the boys back at work when I get back,' he says to himself.

Back on the road, listening to country music on a CD he purchased at the truck stop, he finds himself singing along quite loudly and bursting into laughter, exclaiming, 'I'd make a bloody good country singing star.'

Back at the yard, Michael parks his truck beside a huge old paperbark gum tree. The other guys have no idea why he does this, as his trailer is often scattered with fallen leaves and twigs. This means he has to sweep the debris off the trailer every morning before each load. Jordan is the distribution manager of Kevin Richardson Transport (KRT) and has been with the company for nearly sixteen years. He has seen many people come and go and he is still surprised that Michael has stuck around. It can be a gruelling job sometimes, and the hours can be very long. It's not a suitable job for a devoted family man and that is just what Michael is. He's been married for eighteen years and has two beautiful daughters.

'Hey Jords, you still free in two weeks' time for that fishin' trip?' Michael asks, as he slowly walks towards the office.

'Yeah, Mike, can't wait,' says Jordan. They shorten each other's names, despite the fact that both of them hate it.

'Shit's hot. I am gonna call the company today to book it. We only need one more bloke to fill the numbers, though, and Andy keeps dickin' me around. Ya reckon your son might wanna come along?'

Jordan's son, Danny, works as an IT technician for the company and is a quiet guy. 'Don't see why not,' replies Jords.

'Great, well, have a good weekend and I'll see ya Monday.'

Michael has an unusually wide grin on his face, and just as he turns to walk out of Jordan's office, Jordan catches it in the corner of his eye. He thinks to himself, 'That was a weird grin; it looked kind of evil.' Then he puts that thought away. 'What the hell, it's been a long week and it's time to finish for the day. Head down to the pub and have a few beers with the boys.'

Michael is usually always there, telling a few jokes, but today he isn't. A few guys question if anyone spoke to Michael and found out why he didn't show up. Jordan says, 'I spoke to him but he didn't say anything. Just that he'd see me Monday. He had this evil grin I've never seen before; it kind of gave me the chills.'

The weekend for Michael mainly consisted of family time. It was his oldest daughter's sixteenth birthday, and they had a small party for her. Louise asked him if anything was wrong, as Michael seemed a little distracted, a little out of sorts and not his usual self. Being his wife, she knows every mood and quirk of his, and this was new.

'Nothin's wrong darl', just a long week at work,' he says, as he quickly turns his face away. The urge to kill is enormous and he is fighting it with all he has. There is no way his family can ever become a victim of his evilness; they are the whole reason for all of his remaining sanity. His family sees him as the most loving, caring and kind-hearted man they have ever known. As do his neighbours.

If only they knew.

The birthday candles are blown out and the presents are opened. Michelle is over the moon as she got the latest iPad she was hoping for. All her friends at school have one and she felt left out. Now, of course, she can be part of the group without sitting there feeling stupid. 'Thanks, Daddy, you're the bomb. I love you so much. I'm going to my room to set it all up.'

So, that was the last anyone saw of Michelle until the next day. She didn't even come down for dinner. 'You really outdid yourself, Hun, the look on Michelle's face was priceless. The way her face lit up, she is so happy,' says Louise.

'I adore my kid's love and she has been good, doin' all her chores and stuff, she deserves it,' says Michael, as he goes off into the kitchen to grab his third beer for the day.

The following week saw Michael working deliveries in the Sydney metropolitan area, and due to the busy workload, he completely forgot about the murders. While driving, he listens to talk-back radio, often voicing his points of view out loud. The hourly news is a feature that he usually takes no notice of, 'Blah, blah, blah, nothing but boring crap,' he whinges quietly to himself. This particular day, Thursday, a report caught his interest.

'A body has been found in light scrub just north of Batemans Bay. The remains of the badly decomposed body were found by a bush walker, who by chance took a different path than their usual trek. The identity of the body is yet to be determined by the police.'

'Bugger me! That's the first chick I did. What was her name? Oh yeah, Stephanie,' he recalls. 'That was a while ago now.' This brings a wry smile to his face; a sense of acknowledgement seems to fill him with a renewed pleasure. An overwhelming euphoria washes over him, and at first he is a little scared, uncertain of how to deal with this new emotion. But it doesn't take long to absorb it and continue on with his afternoon.

The drive back to the yard hit a bottleneck due to a three-car accident on the Princess Highway.

'For god's sake, what is with this traffic?' he moans, unaware of the fatality just over the other side of the hill. On the approach to the accident, he begins to feel sorry for the victim of the tragedy. One car is beyond recognition, the result of a small sedan colliding head on with a medium-sized truck. The third vehicle is wedged underneath the rear of the truck, though the driver appears to be okay.

'That's a nasty accident,' says Michael. The gentle side of his nature floods him with sadness for those who suffered from the accident, and suddenly he has forgotten about the news report.

He finally gets back to the yard fifteen minutes late, but that doesn't bother him. He reverses his truck into the usual spot and wanders over to the office, where he files the signed delivery dockets from his day's drops. All the guys, except for Jordan, have gone home for the day, and therefore there is no mention of the murder.

'Hey Mike, you reckon you could start an hour early tomorrow? I have a big drop going to Lithgow,' asks Jordan.

'Sure Jords, what time do you expect me back?'

'If you head out on time, I'd say by around 2:00 p.m. When you get back, put the paperwork on my desk and knock off early,' says Jordan.

'Yeah, no worries, mate. Appreciate that. Might not be at the pub tomorrow night either. Got the mother-in-law coming over,' replies Michael.

'Ha! Good luck with that, ey,' smirks Jordan.

Michael's alarm goes off, and he is up early in a great mood. He kisses Louise on the forehead as he quietly leaves the house. Grateful for the four-cylinder Ford Laser they own, as it is a quiet car. He likes to be considerate of his neighbours, especially when leaving home at four in the morning.

When he gets to work, he finds that his truck is already loaded and the tray has been swept as well.

'Mornin', Jords. Got the paperwork for me?' asks Michael.

'Yeah, Mike, it's on the passenger seat. You might wanna fuel up when you head out, the gauge says you only got a quarter of a tank,' explains Jordan.

'Oh ok, cheers, mate,' says Michael.

Another routine delivery, no hitchhikers and no truck stop. Overall, it was a pretty good day. Light traffic was a blessing today, with very few red lights. He thought that his workday would be so much easier if he was able to start as early as he did today, maybe he'd have a talk to Jordan when he got back.

Having arrived at Lithgow at ten in the morning, he decided to have a walk around town while the truck was being unloaded.

'Hey Rob, where can I get some brekkie round here,' asks Michael.

'Henderson Cake and Pie Shop down on Mort Street make awesome pies, we usually get our morning tea from there. Oh, and they cook a great egg and bacon roll,' says Rob, who is the designated forklift driver at the Lithgow Joinery Factory.

Michael buys an egg and bacon roll and a bottle of coke for his breakfast. His diet is an average one, mainly consisting of fatty foods. His last medical exam showed that he had high cholesterol, a level of 7.6. Through the roof, is what his doctor said, insisting that he takes medication to help reduce it.

Across the road is a lovely tree-filled park that has the town Epitaph, a memorial for the local men who served in many wars overseas. With large scribbly gum trees and various small gardens, a number of seats and a public toilet, it is a beautiful family friendly environment. It's getting rather warm already this morning but Michael loves summer.

So, he finds an empty seat to enjoy his breakfast and watch the world go by. He notices a few pigeons feeding close to his feet, and he nonchalantly kicks his feet outwards to shoo them away, mumbling under his breath that they are nothing but rats with wings. After sitting absent-minded for nearly fifteen minutes, his mobile phone rings, startling him out of a daze where he'd again drifted off thinking about the fishing trip. He honestly cannot remember the last time he had a break from work, excluding the public holidays. He hasn't taken any holidays for over two years. 'I guess I should talk to Louise over the weekend and organise a break away. Maybe go to the Whitsunday Islands, spend a week at the beginning of autumn, just relaxing by the pool or on the beach,' he thinks out loud.

A light bead of sweat has begun to gather on his forehead while sitting in the sun. He absently wipes his brow, then answers the phone.

'Hello, yeah, Rob. A-ha. Ok, I'm on my way now. I'm just around the corner.'

On his way back, he takes notice of a young brunette who is at a quick-paced jog, running late for her T.A.F.E course in child care. He is very tempted to follow her, to perhaps talk to her. Maybe take her for a drive. But today, she is spared his evil hand to live a happy, fulfilled life, totally unaware of how close she came to her life ending that very day.

Instead, Michael walks back to the joinery, where he collects the necessary paperwork for the job and does a walk around the truck to make sure everything is secure. The chocks of timber used for the load, enabling a forklift to pick up the load is scattered along the tray of the truck. So, he gathers them all and neatly piles them up over the axle of the trailer. Using one of the 'dog and chains,' he secures the timber and stores the other three sets of chains in the storage box under the trailer. A quick call to Jordan is a common thing, this way the lines of communication are always open.

'I'm leaving Lithgow now Jords, should be back by around 1:30 p.m.,' says Michael.

'Thanks Mike, see ya when you get back. If I'm not in my office it's because I am in a meeting. Just leave the paperwork on my desk and knock off,' says Jordan.

2

GONE FISHING

– – – – – – –

The alarm bellows at four in the morning, waking Michael from a strange dream. He was walking through a thick forest in the dark of night, the moon full in the sky. There were bodies everywhere, but none of them had any faces. He had to carefully step over each one with the precision of a soldier at war, sneaking through a dugout. If he steps on a body, it will come to life and grab a hold of his leg, trying to drag him down into the darkness that he leaves his victims in.

With a light bead of sweat on his forehead, he slowly climbs out of bed, trying not to wake Louise. They had a late night last night celebrating his brother-in-law's thirty-eighth birthday.

As he quietly shuffles across the bedroom floor to their en-suite, he begins to focus on the early hour of the day and starts a mental checklist. It feels like there is so much to remember. Yet, he doesn't really need to take much with him today. All the fishing gear has been supplied, from the rods and bait to the tackle and nets. A packed lunch is a must in case there isn't enough food on the boat, but a question he has pondered for a few days is just how much beer he should take. After all, he is driving and cannot afford to lose his licence. 'I can always bring the excess, home unless the boys drink it. Two six-packs should be more than enough,' he whispers to himself.

A quick shower and then to get dressed. It's a little cool this morning, and because it's dark outside, he really can't tell if it's overcast or not. 'Hmmm, long shorts. My favourite Bon Jovi T-shirt and a hoodie should be enough,' he thinks out loud, as he fumbles around getting ready. Louise packed him a few ham and mustard sandwiches last night and put them beside the beer in the fridge so he wouldn't forget.

On his way to the jetty, he picks up Frank from his place. Frank is a bit of a heavy drinker and wanted to down quite a few today. Michael doesn't speak to the guys much at work, he prefers to keep a low profile, though when he does get involved in a conversation, there are times where he just won't shut up. But this morning he welcomes the company, the hour-long drive goes quicker with them.

'You know what, Michael; I gotta say that getting us guys together was a brilliant idea. Hell, I don't even care if I don't catch anything, it's just nice to get away from the missus and kids,' says Frank.

'No problems, Frank. What're ya gonna do if you actually catch any fish?' enquires Michael.

'Dunno mate, probably just give it to you guys. I am not much of a fish eater,' says Frank.

A hotted-up Commodore comes screaming out of a side street burning rubber, causing Michael to swerve erratically, and without realising he mutters, and Frank hears him say, 'You crazy fucking idiot. Be grateful I don't catch you and slice ya throat open.' Naturally, the rest of the drive was relatively quiet. Needless to say, Frank decides to keep just a little distance from Michael for the rest of the day. A side of Michael that people don't usually get to see, and it takes Frank quite by surprise.

As they pull up at the car park, they see three others waiting down by the jetty. John, Jordan and Danny are standing near the steps that lead down to where they will be boarding the boat, right beside a sign that indicates the legal sizes for fish catches. They approach with a good morning cheer and Michael asks, 'Has anyone else turned up yet? We're still waiting on Andy, if he shows up at all, and Matt and Davo.'

'I got a call from Andy and he said he's on his way, and Davo is picking up Matt,' says Danny.

'Did anyone think to bring a camera?' asks John.

'Yeah, I did,' replies Jordan.

Then, ten minutes later, the others pull up, and their timing is good. As the boat is leaving in five minutes, it gives them just enough time to get on board and find a position they feel comfortable with. All the rods are set up and ready to go, and the boys put their bags under the rod that they have chosen to use.

The trip takes them a half hour to get to a reef that is well known for yellow-fin tuna. Once they arrive at their destination, they all get themselves ready, making sure they have bait on their hooks. As each of the guys casts out their fishing lines, the skipper cracks open the beers and hands them around. Cheers all round from everyone, and the day begins with the sun just peaking over the horizon. A hint of purple, yellow and pink starts to form in the sky. The heat of the day will soon follow. Matt is the first to get a bite and all heads turn to watch and wait to see what is on the end of the line. It's the first of many, bream, tailor, one very large tuna and a variety of smaller fish that get thrown back in the water. But for Matt, he caught a small stingray.

By 11:30 a.m., the guys agree to move on and find another area to fish after a half hour of not getting any bites at all, not even a nibble. An opportunity to get some lunch and another beer or two. Light bantering is going on, and Michael has gone quiet. Sitting at the back of the boat listening in and not overly impressed. Frank is the type of guy who will push a joke too far and has occasionally ended up in a great argument or even a fist fight. He never has learnt when to quit. Even back at work, Frank will often find an excuse to have a dig at Michael, a snide remark here and there. Of course, Michael chooses to ignore him, which tends to quietly annoy Frank, but every dog has its day. And will that be today that Frank has it coming to him?

The first half of the day saw calm seas. The water was smooth and glistened like glass. After they pulled their lines in and moved to another location, the swell began to pick up, just a little at first. Not even a concern for any of them. Except maybe for John, who was prone to seasickness. Thankfully, he took some tablets before the trip, which, although it made him feel slightly stoned, he was able to hold his own.

More alcohol flowed and the catches were few, but everyone seemed to be having a good time. An hour into fishing at this location, and the swell started getting a little choppy, with the boat rocking to and fro. At one point, Davo slipped on the floor of the boat and fell square on his bum. Laughing his head off he said, 'Look at me, I'm a fish,' as he wiggled around. This brought a raw of laughter from everyone except Michael, who only managed a polite grin.

Michael sees this as a golden opportunity to make his move on Frank. He hides a fishing knife-blade up against the inside of his right hand and makes out that he is collecting some more bait. He gets in behind Frank where nobody can see the blade and waits until the boat rocks to the right, and when it does, he feigns a fall, plunging the knife into Frank's ribcage. To ensure that people on board would think it was an accident, Michael puts on a great act, 'Frank are you ok? Fuck, I'm so sorry. I slipped when the boat rocked.' Blood is everywhere and panic has set in. 'Shit, we have to get back to shore right away. Hey, skipper, call ahead for an ambulance, there's been an accident,' Michael yells.

'It's going to be ok, just hang in there, Frank,' says Jordan.

As soon as the boat docks, the paramedics rush on board, only to discover that Frank has not made it. He passed away halfway back, and there is an air of silence on the boat. Everyone is so shocked that such a tragic accident could happen to them. Frank worked for the company for seven years and was well liked. Sure, he could be a pain in the neck sometimes, but in general he was a good, all-round decent bloke.

'I am going to close the yard down on Monday. I want everyone to take the day off and take time to reflect on how fragile life is,' says Jordan. 'Also, I will contact Frank's family as soon as we get this cleared up. The police will be here soon to take a report of the accident, so everyone stay close by.'

Constable Erickson arrives and starts the process of interviewing everyone individually. Michael plays it really cool when his turn comes. He explains it exactly how he has planned to, that it was a horrible accident while he was reaching for some bait. He had the knife in his hand so that he could cut a small piece of squid, and the boat rocked violently causing him to slip and fall against Frank.

No charges are laid, however, all the guys are asked to make themselves available in case further information is required. The deep-sea fishing company was cleared of all responsibility and liability, though they may need to be called upon for evidence if the case had to go to court.

The following Saturday, a funeral is held and paid for by KRT, the company Frank worked for. It is a lovely service, Frank's son Mario reads the eulogy and has everyone in tears. Even Michael sheds a few tears. He isn't sad that Frank is dead; in fact, he is pleased. But he needs people to see that he is indeed remorseful for the accident, and, so, he fits in quite well. Had he planned to kill Frank on this fishing trip? No, in fact, it didn't occur to him until only minutes before he fulfilled his desire for murder. He sits beside Louise quietly, pondering his murder count. Three bodies and all female, except Frank. He usually favours the young ladies with brunette hair. 'Frank was an exception to my rule, but I cannot sway from my rules and routine,' he thinks to himself. It will complicate matters too much.

After the funeral, a wake is held at the family home of Frank, and everyone from work shows up to continue to pay their respects. Some stories are told of Frank's antics and the things he got up to in life. Only last year, for his fifty-third birthday, Frank went skydiving, and it was being played on the television (TV) with the volume turned all the way down. Michael thinks that it is a shame that his parachute actually opened, as then he wouldn't have been in the position to get him out of his way for good.

'. . . and then he fell from the roof. It was hilarious because he fell on the doghouse he had built only two weeks prior and smashed it. He only ended up with bruising to his right arm and ribs,' says Frank's wife, Marlene. Michael catches this part of the conversation and waits until Marlene is finished.

'My condolences, Marlene, I can't help but feel so horribly bad for this. I feel totally responsible and I'm torn apart. If there is ANYTHING that I can do, and I mean anything, please let me know,' says Michael painfully.

'Oh, Michael, that is very kind of you. I don't blame you. I know that you didn't mean for this to happen. Are you ok?' she asks.

'No, I am not really coping so well, but like all of us, time will help me heal,' says Michael.

The wake goes on until around six in the evening, and for appearance's sake, Michael and Louise are the last to leave. Again, Michael offers his condolences and support.

'Thank you, Michael. I will keep your offer in mind. For now, I have my immediate family who will be staying for a week or two. Thank you both for coming today and for your love and support,' says Marlene.

'We are truly saddened by your loss, call me anytime,' says Louise.

'Thanks again, perhaps in a few days we can meet up for coffee,' suggests Marlene.

'That would be nice. Take care and we'll stay in touch,' replies Louise.

At home, Michael discusses the events with Louise and lets her know that there may be more interviews with the police yet. 'So, if this happens, please keep this low profile with the girls. This is hard enough to deal with and I don't think that the girls need to know too much,' he says.

'Ok, babe, I understand how you feel and will try to keep this away from the girls,' replies Louise.

Suddenly Michael is filled with a sudden rage, but he hides it as best as he can. 'How in hell can she know how I am feeling? Stupid bitch has absolutely no idea,' he thinks to himself. 'One day they will all know what I am capable of. One day.'

The next day there is a huge thunderstorm, in fact, it woke the whole family, and the girls come running into the bedroom. 'It's ok, just another typical summer storm,' says Michael. He has no idea where this thought came from, but the timing is perfect. 'I've been thinking that the school holidays are coming up in about five weeks. Who wants to spend a week on the Whitsunday Islands? he asks.

Well, that was a great distraction from the storm, and, suddenly, there is light chatter from all three females in the house. He felt outnumbered sometimes.

'Oh, Daddy, for real? That would be like totally awesome,' says Danielle.

Michelle's face lights up and she asks, 'Can I bring Derek?'

'No, sweetie, I think Dad just wants it to be a family affair,' says Louise.

'So, it's agreed? A week on the Whitsundays?' Michael asks. 'All in favour say aye.'

'Aye!' Everybody is in favour of the holiday and he has maintained a happy family facade. Again. On Thursday morning, Michael is woken from a light sleep by a thud at the front door. A sound he would normally recognise and yet he is puzzled by this. 'Who in hell would be at the front door this hour of the morning,' he quietly says, as he turns to look at the alarm clock beside the bed. 'It's bloody well six in the morning,' he says as he slides out of bed. He looks across to see Louise who is fast asleep and even lightly snoring. 'And she goes off at me for snoring,' he laughs. Under his side of the bed, he has a baseball bat within easy reach for matters of protection. They were burgled two years ago while they were home, and since then Michael has amped up the security around the house. He installed a back-to-base alarm system and also put up a few sensor floodlights to ward intruders off. He is still thinking of installing small security cameras around the perimeter of the house, the kind that you can access from your mobile phone. So, with his slippers on and the baseball bat in his right hand, he quietly approaches the front door.

'Hello, anyone there?' enquires Michael. Nothing. Not a sound. He gently opens the door to find the local newspaper, rolled up in plastic, lying at his feet. Feeling a little stupid, he picks up the paper, steps out onto the front steps and has a look around the front yard anyway, then goes back in closing the door behind him.

A van makes this same delivery every Thursday, tossing the paper out of the window of the passenger seat. He has a partner to do this, it would be far too dangerous to throw newspapers and drive at the same time. Usually the paper will end up in the garden or the middle of the driveway, but this morning it's a direct hit.

'That's four in a row,' says the passenger. 'One more and I win the bet, ten bucks you'll owe me,' he says.

The driver retorts with, 'Yeah, ok, smart arse.'

'Well, I'm up now. May as well put the jug on,' Michael says. He is fortunate to have a late start today. Only a few local deliveries, so he had been hoping for a sleep in. Of course, there is no such luck. After making his first coffee for the day he unravels the paper and does his best to flatten it out. He rolls it in reverse. His obsessive-compulsive disorder (OCD) kicks in, and he finds it slightly annoying that the paper is still a little dishevelled. Still, he manages to get it straight enough so that it is easy enough to flick through.

The front-page headline reads, 'Man dies while fishing.' He is curious to read what the authorities have to say about it and begins reading when Danielle comes shuffling into the kitchen.

'Morning, Daddy.' mumbles Danni.

'Good morning, sweetie, want some breakfast?' he asks, but can see that she already has her head buried in the fridge, like any typical teenager.

'Honey, close the door unless you are actually going to get something out,' he says. Just as he has finished saying this, she closes the door and has a large juice bottle in her hand.

'What time do you start work today, Daddy?' she asks, while pouring a glass of Orange Mango juice.

'Ten o'clock. Why?' he replies.

'Could you drive me to school, please?'

The school is on his way to work and he doesn't mind being a little early to work. 'Sure can, sweetie. Do you need any money for lunch, my shout today.' he asks.

'Gee thanks, Dad, that'd be great. Is ten dollars too much to ask for?' she shyly asks.

'I think I can spare that,' he says, while sipping his coffee.

Michael goes back to reading the newspaper and isn't surprised to find that the story is low-key. It simply tells of a man accidentally stabbed on board a deep-sea fishing boat just outside the heads from Sydney harbour. The man died on board before reaching shore and no charges were laid, though further investigations are being considered. The article also went on to advise the reader of the dangers fishing sometimes presented, with as many as nine deaths in the last twelve months.

On page five, there is a small article about the body that was found just north of Batemans Bay. Forensic evidence is still being gathered from the area; also, the police are waiting on the results of a DNA test in order to identify the body. Nobody has come forth with any helpful information, and a missing person's report is being investigated.

Michael gets up from the kitchen counter with a grin and goes to have a shower. He has a very unusual look on his face that makes Danielle feel just a little uncomfortable. She has never seen a creepy look on her father's face before and she puts it down to the recent stress that he has been under. Brushing the creepy moment aside, she goes back into her bedroom to start getting ready for school.

They leave home at a quarter past eight and arrive at Danielle's high school at 8:40 a.m. One part of the day Michael thoroughly enjoys, as he rarely gets to spend that little extra time with his girls. Besides, the senior girls at the high school are quite nice to watch walking around. Most are still a little young for his new-found hobby, so he likes to think of it. But in a few years' time they will be suitable prey. He kisses Danni on the cheek and wishes her a wonderful day, then drives off to work. He does get to work early and lucky he does, as there are a couple of more deliveries added to his workload.

When he arrived, there was a police car in the visitor's car park, and he naturally thought that it had to do with Frank's untimely death. If only it was that simple. The police found a delivery docket, though badly faded, at the crime scene of the recently discovered body.

3

THE FIRST TIME

September 12, a young girl went missing on her way to visit a best friend who not so long ago moved to Ulladulla, south of Wollongong. She was supposed to arrive shortly before lunchtime, but she never showed. Her best friend Karen waited until five in the afternoon and then phoned this girl's parents.

'Hi there, Mrs. Sampson, it's Karen. Has Stephanie left home yet? I was expecting her around lunchtime, but she hasn't turned up. Also, she isn't answering her phone,' says Karen. Alarm bells immediately go off for Mrs. Sampson as it is completely uncharacteristic of Stephanie not to have at least called someone.

'Oh, hello, Karen, yes, Stephanie left at ten this morning and was getting a train to Wollongong, where she was then supposed to have organised a lift with a friend,' says Mrs. Sampson.

'I'm really worried about her, should I call the police?' asks Karen.

'No, it's alright. I will make a few phone calls and see if she hasn't gone to her cousin's place. I'll call you back, in, say, half an hour, and we can go from there,' says Mrs. Sampson.

Karen is feeling very uncomfortable and edgy about this and cannot sit still. Instead, she paces the hallway floor where the home phone sits attached to the wall just near the lounge room door. Minutes feel like hours, and hours feel like days.

Finally, Mrs. Sampson phones back. 'Nobody has heard from her, Karen. I'm really worried now. I am now going to call the police and file a missing person's report. If you hear of anything, please call me straight away, please.' pleads Mrs. Sampson.

'Yes, of course, I will. God! I hope she is ok,' replies Karen.

That was the last time she was seen alive, when her mother took her to Central Station to get the train.

Michael is on his way to Batemans Bay with a large load of timber and decides to stop at Ulladulla for lunch. He wasn't so lucky with parking his truck anywhere close to the small shops at the main street. He had to walk two blocks to get onto the main street, and when he gets there he finds a seafood place. 'Looks good enough to me,' he says and wanders on in.

'G'day, mate, what'll it be?' says the old guy behind the counter.

After a quick look at the menu board above the cookers and fryers, Michael orders a lunch special, which consists of one piece of fish, some calamari rings, seafood stick and hot chips. 'Can I get some tartar sauce with it, mate,' he asks.

'Yeah, no worries, be ready in about ten for ya, mate,' replies the old bloke.

Bottle of coke, hot seafood and a gorgeous spring day, what more could he ask for. Across the road is a park joined to the boat ramp where locals set off for a day of recreational activities. Michael walks over to the rock wall and sits down to enjoy his lunch. Soon after, a small boat glides in with the motor idling. The two guys on board are shuffling about in preparation for a gentle grinding halt into the sand just before the concrete ramp.

As the pelicans are floating across the sky, they are watching the boat pulling into the shore in anticipation of a feed. It is quite common for people to clean their catch at the council provided wash bench, and the scraps get tossed aside. Feeding time is anytime fish are gutted and cleaned and its always a fun sight to see, sometimes the pelicans will fight over the scraps; with their long bills they lock into each other momentarily, and, as usual, the dominant bird wins over.

This got Michael thinking about the dominance he likes to have over the weaker people he has known in his life. After years as a child watching his father often beat his mum, for sometimes no reason, he has tried fervently not to walk in his father's footsteps. 'We all have our weaknesses from time to time,' he assures himself. And it doesn't excuse this behaviour, but sometimes they deserve it, they need to be put in their place. Having this type of mood swings and aggression can be quite a challenge to hide, as he prefers to live a quiet, happy life.

He really should be getting back on the road. He still has to deliver this timber and be back in Smithfield by 5:00 p.m. He is a little fastidious about cleanliness and is not in the habit of leaving a mess behind, so he collects his remains from lunch and discards them into the closet bin he can find. Satisfied with himself, he quietly begins whistling a tune of no particular song. Just the happy whistle of a content man.

Back on the road and only a few minutes into driving, Michael can see ahead of him what appears to be a young woman hitchhiking. So, he begins to slow the truck and is able to pull up beside her. He leans across the passenger seat and opens the door.

'Where are you headed?' he asks her.

'Batemans Bay to see a friend. How far are you going?' she asks.

'Matter of fact, I am going to Batemans Bay. Climb in,' he says.

'Hi there, my name is Stephanie, what's yours?' she asks.

'Michael. So, what's in the bay for you?' he asks.

'Oh, I am going to stay with my best friend who moved there four months ago,' she said.

'Sounds nice, how long have you known each other?'

'Since primary school, then we were lucky enough to go to the same high school. She moved to be with her boyfriend. I don't particularly like him, he's an arrogant prick,' said Stephanie.

After a little more idle chatting, they both continue the journey in silence, when after only ten minutes of driving, there is a loud bang from under the truck. Of course, Michael knows the exact cause; they ran over a large branch that fell from the trees hanging over the road.

'Shit, what was that?' asked Stephanie.

'I don't know but I will have to pull over to check it out. Feel free to get out and stretch your legs,' says Michael.

As Michael is inspecting the truck, Stephanie wanders over to a native flower growing beside the road. Michael picks up the steel bar he keeps on the tray and quietly walks up behind her, and with as much force as he could, he hits Stephanie across the back of the head. Not satisfied with just the one hit, he continues to hit her in the head until her skull in practicality caves in. He lights up a cigarette and smokes until he calms down.

Unbeknownst to him, as Stephanie got out of the truck, a loose delivery docket falls from the passenger door and floats under the truck. He crushes out his cigarette, then picks up Stephanie carrying her about fifty metres into the scrub. He finds a variety of twigs, branches and leaves and covers the body. Once he is satisfied that visually she won't easily be seen, he confidently walks back to the truck and continues on with his day as usual.

Upon arriving at his destination, he feels this sense of fulfilment. An overwhelming boost of confidence surrounds him, and he is in a very light and jovial mood. Thankfully, no one at this factory has ever met him before and just thinks he's a cheerful bloke. Later on, when some of the investigations start becoming frequent, this will work in his favour. Naturally, this is something that will never occur to him, even when he is interviewed by detectives about the discoveries; he will maintain a light and happy disposition.

Strangely, as he drives back to work and has to travel the same roads back, he pauses briefly at the very spot where he left Stephanie – he is almost compelled to pull over, just to make sure that what happened wasn't a weird dream. Also, he was mildly curious if someone happened to walk past – as he noticed a walking track through the bush land just metres away from the incident – how hard it would be to see her. He can't do anything about it now, so his journey continues.

With a slight feeling of remorse, barely noticeable in fact, he decides not to pay it any more attention and to put it behind him. Until another opportunity presents itself, he goes about his routine with his work and family life like nothing bad has ever happened.

The following few murders happen in a similar fashion. He finds the occasional hitchhiker amidst warm weather and long-distance driving. He enjoys the company and hearing the stories of those he picks up. One hitchhiker was going to Byron Bay to a small festival being held there. Lots of alternative music and dope smoking would've been on the agenda for this three-day event. But not everyone falls victim to his heavy hand, most are just travelling around and he's happy to help them get closer to their destination.

There have been times when he has picked up a hitchhiker and had the urge to kill, but he has a preference for young women, sandy blonde/brunette hair and quite attractive. Of course, that is not so easy to find when he's travelling, as most of the people he sees are guys in the mid to late twenties, guys who could take care of themselves. He isn't a silly man; he knows that if he tried his luck against a moderately built man, he would not achieve what he set out to do. He feels better when he has control of the situation. So, it goes without saying that the weaker and more vulnerable people are the right recipe for murder.

4

QUESTIONS

Two weeks have passed since Frank's death and so far there has been no real rush by local police to investigate any further. So, why were the police at his house this afternoon when he got home from work? As he slowly approaches his house, he tries to recall the events that happened on the boat. 'Fairly easy to remember,' he says, 'no sweat.' Though a little case of nerves rushes over him and he pulls the car over three houses away. 'Ok, big fella, take a deep breath and relax. They probably just have to ask a few questions to finalise the case before closing it,' he reassures himself.

A few minutes pass, and he then drives the rest of the way home full of confidence, as if someone had switched a light on. He gets out of his car and locks it behind him, just another security measure he has after the break-in. One never knows who is watching and when. With a confident stride he walks to the front door and lets himself in, knowing full well the door would be unlocked.

'Hi, honey, do you remember Constable Erickson? He says that he spoke to you a couple of weeks ago about Frank?' asked Louise.

'Oh, yeah, how are you, officer? What can I do for you?' he asks. 'Is this about frank?'

'As a matter of fact, no. That case was closed last week. An unfortunate accident too – poor family is still grieving. I spoke to his wife a few days ago. Guess it will be a while for the pain to heal,' said Constable Erickson.

'Oh, ok. So, what is this about?' asked Michael. Keeping that look of confidence on his face, but playing it smart, he knows not to start to look worried. Though internally, he is quite puzzled by this visit. He cannot think for the life of him why he would want to be questioned then.

'We are only asking questions at this point in time, and as I haven't been able to get you at work, I figured it would be easier to see you at home. That is unless you would prefer to come down to the station for questioning,' said the cop.

'No, no I am fine here. So, what's this about?' he asked.

'Have you heard the report of a body found just north of Batemans Bay?' asked the Constable.

'Yeah, I briefly heard about it on the radio while driving the other day,' he replied. 'What about it?'

'Well we found a delivery docket near the crime scene that has a letter head from the company that you work for. Do you ever go down that way to do deliveries?' he asked.

'Sure, a few of us have over time. But how is it linked to the murder? I guess it is possible a docket flew out the window while driving,' says Michael.

'Well like I said, we are just asking questions for now. The docket has a date on it that coincides with an approximate time for the death of this person. Early September. Do you recall driving down that way then?' he asks.

'I recall at least three deliveries in September down that way,' says Michael. 'I can't say I remember seeing anything out of the norm.'

'Did you see a young girl walking along the road, possibly hitchhiking?' asked the Constable.

'Sorry, I think I'd remember seeing someone walking along that road. There are some remote spots out that way and with no street lights, I'd hate to break down there,' says Michael.

'Ok, well, if you think of anything please give me a call. Here's my card,' said Constable Erickson as he pulls a card from his identification wallet.

'I certainly will, sorry, I couldn't be of any more help. I'll talk with the guys at work too. Maybe we can help in some way,' Michael said. With that said the officer saw his way out and left.

'That was strange how he came to the house instead of your work, Michael, did you know he'd been asking questions?' asked Louise.

'Yeah it was strange, but then again with me being on the road so often he might not have been able to make a time to see me at work and would have found it easier to see me here. He'd have our address from the information I gave him about Frank,' said Michael. He unintentionally avoided answering her question and said that he was going to have a shower; it had been quite hot in the truck today.

'Ok, Hun, dinner will be ready in half an hour. Also, the girls are having a sleep over with one of their friends from school, so we have the house to ourselves tonight,' she said.

After dinner, they sat and watched her favourite reality TV show *So You Think You Can Cook*. A show where average people compete against each other with their own recipes. The judges have no say in what will be cooked each night but do make suggestions. Each night one person gets eliminated from the show, and out of fourteen people, the last two have to cook something that the judges want. This show bores the hell out of Michael, but as he loves his wife so much he doesn't mind sitting with her. He enjoys spending time with her – being very busy at work lately he feels that he doesn't spend enough time with her – small price to pay for genuine love.

After the show finishes they both go to bed and make passionate love for a while before falling asleep in each other's arms. Michael wakes at 1.15 a.m. from a horrible dream. He had been kidnapped as a small boy and sold off to a family living in another state. When he arrived at his new home, there were weird spider-like people with whips who would make hundreds of children do lots of digging. When he looked into the holes he saw dead bodies. What woke him so violently was one face he saw when looking in those holes. It was his face as an adult. He got up to go to the toilet, then came back to bed and cuddled up to Louise whispering in her ear, 'I love you so much, I'm sorry babe.' Louise stirred a little then resumed her light snoring. Totally unaware he said anything at all.

The next morning, both of them got up and had breakfast together, something that they don't often have a chance to do and haven't done so in a long time. 'We should do this more often,' Michael says.

'I totally agree, how quiet is it without the girls? I miss them, though,' says Louise.

'Did you sleep well last night? I felt you stirring a lot. I even thought I heard you say that you were sorry,' she says.

'I did have a weird dream that woke me, but I can't remember what it was. And I don't recall talking, must have been a part of the dream,' he says.

'Suppose so. Will you be home late tonight? I want to talk more about our holiday. The girls have two weeks of school holidays next month, and I thought that we should make the arrangements soon,' says Louise.

'I'm not sure what I have on today. The list I saw yesterday afternoon indicates all local deliveries, so I should be home at a reasonable time. If you get a chance today, could you grab a few brochures please?' he politely asked.

That night, the family sat at the dinner table discussing what they'd like to do on their holidays. Danielle wants to go snorkelling and do lots of swimming, while Michelle just wants to sit by the pool listening to her iPod and playing games on her iPad.

'Boring,' Danielle chuckled. The parents are just happy to do whatever the girls want, though quietly Michael wouldn't mind having one day alone to do some fishing, or maybe take his new Nikon out and do a little photography.

'Ok, well, I have an idea,' says Michael. 'How about we all write down all the things that we want to do, mum can put a salad bowl on the kitchen bench, and by Thursday we can sit down and go through the list. I'll leave these brochures here so that you can see some of the activities they have, and then put together an itinerary.'

'That's a great idea, Dad,' says Michelle. Louise just smiles and gives Michael a kiss on the cheek. She gets up and starts cleaning up after dinner, stacking the dishes and rinsing as she goes. The girls go to their room and are quietly discussing their ideas for fun in the sun. Michael decides to help out in the kitchen; he would normally just go off and watch TV. Tonight, however, he feels that he can use this opportunity to bond a little more with his beautiful wife.

'After we have sorted out what we all would like to do, I am going to take Monday off work and make all of the arrangements. I think a hut style cabin sounds like a good idea,' says Michael. 'That's a great idea, Hun. I like the idea of something different. Also, no technology, although Michelle wants to bring a few things,' says Louise.

'Yeah, I know, I suppose we can allow that. If it makes her happy and keeps the peace, I can't see any harm in it,' he says.

Saturday night arrives and there is a lot of discussion going on, and at one time, a little arguing between the two girls.

'Alright, enough of that, you too, or I'll make you do each other's things there. I have enough information to sort the rest out with your mother,' says Michael.

'Yes, Girls, your father and I will sort it out and make sure you get to have fun,' says Louise. With that, the girls get up and leave the table mumbling to each other. Michael and Louise cannot understand what they were saying but have a fair idea.

The following day, Michael confirms with payroll that his annual leave has been approved. 'Hey Jords, you still ok with me taking time off?' asks Michael.

'Yeah, no sweat. We got your deliveries covered. Just have a good time, huh,' replies Jordan.

'Oh, I am going to, you can bet on that,' says Michael.

Again, with a weird smile. Not a happy smile. Somehow, it looked a little sinister. At least that was the impression that Jordan got, he could have read it wrong.

'Oh yeah Mike, before you go, I need to chat with you in my office,' Jordan says.

'Oh ok, just gimmie five minutes and I'll be there,' replies Michael.

'So, what did you want to see me for?' asks Michael.

'I've had the police come here three times this week asking questions, something to do with a delivery docket found near a body discovered down south,' says Jordan. 'They have a rough time frame for when the body was left there, and the date given on the docket indicates that you did the deliveries that week.'

'Yeah, they came by my place the other night asking me about it, what about it?' asked Michael.

'I'm just a little curious about it. You are normally quite pedantic about your paperwork, yet you never mentioned losing a docket,' explains Jordan.

'To be honest, I don't recall losing any dockets, then or ever,' says Michael. 'I don't know what else to tell you, I've already spoken with the cops about this.'

'Ok, well if you think of anything that could help the police I'd appreciate it. It doesn't look good having a police car on the premises when we have clients coming and going,' says Jordan.

'I totally agree with you. Sorry it has caused discomfort but I will certainly be cooperative. I don't really see any connection with our company and this situation, so hopefully, it will blow over soon,' says Michael.

Michael leaves Jordan's office feeling quite annoyed. As if he was being accused of something, and though he is responsible for this problem, he is not ready to stop his killing, not yet anyway. If things got out of hand and he was arrested, he would be forced to stop. The question is, though, whether or not he would confess to any other murders. He doubts that he will, but when backed into a corner, he has no idea how he'd react.

'Dammit, I need to go for a drive to cool off and gather myself, get under control,' he quietly says. On his way home after just cruising around, he is pulled onto a roadside Random Breath Test. 'More police, what is it with the cops lately,' he thinks as he comes to a stop.

'Evenin', officer. How goes it?' he asks jovially.

'Have you had anything to drink this afternoon?' asked the police officer, quite bluntly. The cop is at the end of his shift and has had to arrest four drivers in the last hour. His mood is very short, and Michael quickly picks up on this and decides to just go with the process and avoid small talk.

'Not today, officer,' he says.

'Please count into the device until I tell you to stop,' says the officer.

'Stop, do you have your licence on you?'

Michael did and handed it to the officer who informed him that he will be back in a moment. Just another situation for Michael to feel annoyed. The officer was gone for only a few minutes; however, it seemed a lot longer than that. Upon his return, the officer says, 'You're free to go, drive safely.'

With that said and done, Michael felt defeated and simply drove home to hopefully a peaceful night.

'Tomorrow is Friday and a few beers at the pub with the boys sounds like a good idea,' he says as he pulls into his driveway.

'Hi sweetheart, sorry I am later than I expected to be. I had a meeting with Jordan about that case the cops are investigating,' he says.

'That's ok, darling, I've only just finished preparing dinner. Go wash up and call the girls,' says Louise.

That night was as he'd hoped it would be. It was quiet and relaxing; a renovation show that Michael likes to watch was on and the girls were in their rooms doing homework. Louise was reading the latest Janet Donovan novel about a love twist between two sisters. All was good in the Hubert household.

5

TAKE OFF

- - - - - - -

It felt like this moment would never come for Michael. The alarm is set for five in the morning, and excitedly he jumps out of bed. The night before he made sure that everyone's luggage was packed and ready to go. He went in to wake his girls and get them up; each one will need to have a quick shower.

'Good morning, Girls. Time to rise and shine,' he says. While he was saying this he had a flashback to his younger years, as this is how his mother would wake him most weekends. 'And please don't be too long in the shower, your mum and I need to shower as well. We need to be out the front door no later than 8:00 a.m., so no dilly-dallying around.'

'Ok, Dad,' both girls say in unison.

Michael goes back into his bedroom and Louise is already up and fiddling about.

'Mornin', Hun. I slept like a rock, which surprised me considering how much I am looking forward to this break. Did you sleep ok?' asks Louise.

'Surprisingly, I slept ok too,' he replies.

After everyone has showered and dressed, they all help in loading up the car. They then have a light breakfast before leaving for the airport. On the road by 8:15 a.m. and thankfully the traffic is moderate, they should make it to the airport by 9:30 a.m.

'Dad, can I sit next to the window on the plane?' asks Danielle.

'I am not sure where we're sitting until we check in, but I will ask when we get there,' Michael replies.

'Thanks, Daddy,' she says and goes back to the game on her iPod. The radio is on a morning breakfast show and the DJs talk endlessly, Michael finds their incessant chatter frustrating. With many breakfast shows, there is a brief news break and a traffic update, so at 8:30 a.m. when the news comes on and Michael is about to flick through the channels, there is a report about another body that was found recently by a farmer from Bulahdelah.

'I was mendin' me fences yesterdee aftanoon,' says the farmer, 'and me dog Rex wouldn't stop barken, he was going crazy until I came ova ta see what he was goin' on about, and that's when I found her.' The reporter asked if he'd seen or heard anything suspicious lately. 'Nah, I woulda rung the cops if I did,' he said. The body was covered in leaves and branches and was badly decomposed. 'There were some items nearby that may be linked to the body but as of now the police are not saying if they have a positive ID or a motive yet. 'We'll hopefully have more soon. Bryan Rogers for 2FLA-FM news,' says the reporter.

'How horrible, that's the second body in two weeks,' says Louise.

'Yeah, I think what is happening in this world is sad, people killing each other. There needs to be more love and kindness. Otherwise what's the point?' Michael says.

'I hear that,' says Michelle. 'Just the other day there was like this huge fight at school and this girl got her arm broken. It was like totally awful.'

'You never mentioned anything, was she a friend of yours?' asks her mum.

'I didn't say anything because I like totally forgot about it, and, no, it was that skank, Sharon Dixon,' says Michelle.

'LANGUAGE,' her dad exclaims.

'Sorry, Dad, but she is. She's always picking on other kids and being noisy in class. She is a pain in the . . .'

'I think we get the point Michelle,' her mum says.

The rest of the drive was a quiet one. Michael switched the radio off and tries to fight off a tense mood – one he associates with the emotions that run through him just before he kills someone.

When they arrive at the airport, they go straight to the parking station where they will leave the car while they are away. While Michael is taking the luggage out of the car, Louise goes to get a luggage trolley, thank goodness, she has her purse with her and has small change in it. 'A two-dollar fee to unlock a trolley! Gee! They'll charge for anything,' moans Louise.

Back to the car, and she finds that all the bags are neatly stacked on the ground. She never did understand Michael's OCD nature but never chipped at him about it. She'd rather a tidy helpful husband, than a slovenly, lazy pig of a man. A few minutes pass and the trolley is stacked, ready to go.

'Ok, now we need to check our bags in, and if that does not take too long, we should have about fifty minutes before we are called to board the plane. I would like to get a coffee, maybe something for you guys, and then have a browse around the overpriced shops, sound good to you?' Michael asks. They all agree and then head for the check-in line.

Jetaway Airlines are running approximately twenty-five minutes late due to heavy fog in Melbourne and make an announcement apologising for the delay. Of course, this didn't bother the Hubert family, it just gave them more time to stroll around and relax. Half an hour later, the family made their way to gate sixteen where they sat in the waiting area until the announcement was made to board the plane.

There is a seventy-two inch HDTV up on the wall with a satellite pay-per-view news channel on. So, with little else to do save for his wife and children, who are occupied with either a book or an electronic device, Michael sits slouched and watches a news report on yet another bombing in Afghanistan. Rebels have attacked a peaceful town and blown up the American Consulate building, killing ninety officials and civilians, plus wounding thirty-four others. According to the local authorities, three car bombs were used to detonate the explosives, and Al-Qaeda are rumoured to be the attackers.

Michael has a weak moment after seeing that report where he feels guilty of those that he has murdered. How could he be so horrible, isn't there enough death in this world? 'Obviously not,' he mumbles.

'What, Hun?' asked Louise.

'Huh? Oh, nothing. I was just thinking out loud, watching the bombing overseas,' he says.

'Oh, ok,' she replies and goes back to reading her book.

That feeling doesn't last long, as for his own reality, he can't help that he has that evil desire to kill. It's a pleasure that he will never be able to explain to any rational being.

'Passengers for flight JA317, please board through gate sixteen, seats forty through to twenty-six are asked to board first. Please make sure that you have your tickets ready to be scanned,' it is announced. Michael rechecks the tickets and notes that their tickets are 16A, B, C and D. He is grateful that on the plane they all get to sit close to one another and the girls get a window each. They only have to wait another twelve minutes before the announcement is made for them to board the plane. This is the first time the girls have ever been on a plane, and the walk down the corridor, to the entrance door of the plane is exciting. The look on their faces warm their mother's heart and fill her with delight.

The plane is on the runway fifteen minutes later and the lift off is so exciting that Danielle lets out a little squeal. Michelle is taking photos of the airfield as the plane roars down the runway. Both the girls are enthralled by the whole experience but Louise is mildly nervous. It is her first flight as well, and she had no idea just how powerful a plane could be.

Michael was born in Queensland, and when he was seventeen, against his will, his family moved to Sydney. They had all of their furniture and goods moved by truck, and they flew from Brisbane airport. He also had to fly back to Brisbane for a funeral, a couple of years before he met Louise. His grandfather died from cancer; he'd been smoking all his life and it finally caught up to him. So, of course, flying isn't such a big deal for him, but he does get a lot of enjoyment from seeing his family so excited and happy. Oh, how he truly loves them.

Michael finds it fascinating being above the clouds, though this time he is happy for his daughters to experience this amazing sight. The colours of the land vary in many different shades of green with almost symmetrical squares dividing the farms. Then, flying over the Great Dividing Range, it becomes apparent to Michelle just how vast and thick it is. She remembers doing an assignment on this last year for her geography class, and at the time, she thought it was just a narrow line of bush.

'Hey, Mum, check out the bush land below. It goes for miles and miles,' she says.

Her mum, still nervous, takes a quick glance and says nervously, 'Wow, you're right, it's very pretty, isn't it?' As a matter of fact, it was very beautiful.

Michelle then suddenly realised what she wants to do when she leaves school – travel Australia. 'Hey, Dad?' she says.

'Yes, Princess?' says her father.

'I am old enough now to get a job. When we get back from the holidays I want to look for a part-time job. So, I can save up and see Australia. Do a little travel and then go to uni after that. Can I?' she asks, fluttering her eyelids. She knows it makes her dad turn to mush.

'I think it's a good idea, BUT, if it starts to affect your grades, you will quit and concentrate on school. For now, let's just say that it is a yes and we can talk more about this when we get home,' he says.

'Deal, I promise,' she says, and puts her hand out to shake in agreement.

The flight takes a little over an hour and is a direct one to Hamilton Island. Here the family get off the plane, onto the tarmac, which creates more excitement for the girls, Louise included. A fifteen-minute wait inside the small airport is all that is required before their luggage comes around on the luggage carousel, and once they have everything, it is then a short taxi ride to the wharf, for the boat road across to Whitsunday Island.

Choppy seas made for a very bumpy ride, and they are all extremely glad to get off the boat. Louise's bottom is sore from bouncing up and down on the hard plastic seat and is happier than anyone else. The girls are far too excited to notice, and Michael is used to the rough waters due to a number of fishing trips in the past, so he knew how to ride with the waves and bumps.

When they arrive at the shore of the island resort, there are staff waiting to greet them. One of them organises everybody's bags and has them sent to their rooms. Another escorts them to the reception desk. This is done so that their clients don't fumble around struggling with their bags and trying to find where to check in – all part of the experience of Manuka Resort. The check-in only takes about five minutes, handy because Michael had organised all the necessary information with them prior.

Their hut style accommodation is very welcoming with chocolates on the bed. A very relaxed atmosphere, with big palm trees outside, and a hammock just out in front of the hut. Inside there is a bunk bed for the girls – Danielle calls shotgun for the top bunk, much to Michelle's dislike – a double bed for the parents and a small serviced kitchenette. While Michael unpacks he is thinking of making a coffee when he is done before going out to have fun.

'Lunch is at twelve and I thought it would be nice if we had a quick look around and see what things they have to do, then go to the restaurant and have a good meal,' says Michael.

'What are you saying? That my meals aren't good?' Louise says.

It's not like her to be in a snappy mood, thinks Michael, so he quickly replies with, 'Oh, Hun, you make the best meals. I just think you deserve having someone cook for you. God knows I don't cook enough at home.'

That got him out of hot water. 'That's sweet and true. Sorry if I snapped. I just don't feel so great,' Louise says.

'That is quite ok, Bub, is there anything I can get you?' he asks.

'No, I am fine. Probably just an upset tummy from the boat ride,' she says. What Michael doesn't know is that for the past six months, Louise has been drinking during the day, and she hasn't had a drink in two days, so she is feeling a little edgy.

The whole family goes on a walk and enjoys the tropical breeze coming off the ocean. It is a very warm day and Danielle suggests that they all go swimming after lunch.

'That's a great idea, Sweetie,' her dad says.

'Maybe we can play Marco Polo,' says Danielle.

'Sounds good to me,' says mum.

So, after lunch that is what they do. Michelle isn't overly keen but does join in for a little while, until she gets bored and quietly gets out of the pool, wraps a towel around her hair and sits down on a banana chair with her tunes.

The holidays are starting off quite nicely.

6

THE INCIDENT

‘I thought I might go out and do some photography on my own tomorrow, Babe, would you mind?' asks Michael. After he'd spent the last two days doing activities with the family, like snorkelling and beach volleyball, he needed some alone time, and besides, it had been far too long since he took his camera gear for a workout.

'That's fine, Michael. The girls and I are probably just going to sit around the pool and relax, so go off and have fun,' Louise says. Again, Louise sounded flat and it has Michael just a little concerned, but he just put it down to lady stuff. He could never remember when she was due and just figured that she was at that particular time in the month, so it's best not to push his luck with anything.

'Thanks, Bub, you're the best,' he says.

Just then, Danielle comes running inside saying Michelle has twisted her ankle and cannot walk. Immediately, Michael goes into protection mode and flies out the door with Danielle right behind him.

'She's on the tennis courts, Dad' she says.

When they get there, he discovers that a young guy has his arm around his daughter and yells, 'Get away from her.' The poor young guy looks terrified and immediately steps out of the way.

'Dad, I'm fine. This is Wayne and we were playing tennis when my foot slipped and I fell,' says Michelle.

'Are you sure you are ok?' Michael asks.

'Yes, Daddy, I am ok. My ankle hurts but it will settle down. I think I sprained it a little. I'll put an ice pack on it when we get back to the room,' she says.

'Ok, here, grab my hand,' her father says.

'So, who was the boy?' her father asks, as he attends to her swelling ankle.

'I told you, Daddy, that was Wayne. He is here with his parents, just like us. They live in Sydney, his dad is a finance broker,' she explains.

'Oh ok. Just be careful, ok, sweetheart?' he says.

'Yes, Daddy, I will,' she replies.

That night at dinner, Michael catches Michelle and Wayne giving each other coy smiles and thinks to himself, 'Young love, I remember those days.' He may even go and introduce himself to that boy's family, but for now he's happy to keep it until tomorrow night.

The next morning at breakfast, Wayne and his family are walking into the restaurant as the Hubert's are walking out and he catches Michelle blowing Wayne a kiss. Naturally, as any father in his position would be, he isn't impressed and feels that he might just have to keep a close eye on that boy.

Meanwhile, it will have to wait; it's time for some photography. Michael had packed his gear the night before and made sure that he put the camera battery on charge. They were staying on the eastern side of the island and Michael thought he would venture to the western side. His plan was to take his time heading out, stopping whenever something caught his eye, and be on the other side in time for a, hopefully, beautiful sunset.

He also made sure that his mobile phone was fully charged – if he got into trouble he was going to need it. The last thing that he wanted was to be walking along and to suddenly fall down a ravine. Besides he was expecting at some point, for his wife to call and check to see how he was doing. Though with her mood lately he wondered if she really would. Maybe she wanted some time for herself.

Around the back of the resort's main office there is a walking track, and along the way there are a few other tracks that meander off in different directions. At the reception desk there is a wide variety of brochures and maps of the island, offering lots of activities, including wakeboarding. The maps are very easy to follow, and you don't need to inform any of the staff that you are going for a hike. That's why the maps are so easily laid out. There is no way that anybody could get themselves lost.

Before he sets off, up the track, he stops to attach his camera to the tripod and also clicks the shutter release cable into place. This way he is prepared for any shot. Along the walk, he is fascinated by the amazing flora, the wild ferns and vines that are intertwined through many trees. The sun would shine through the trees in unusual places, creating streams of light. A great photo opportunity was in this area and he spends quite a while taking photos, including a number of macro shots. When he totally relaxes his mind and starts to focus on his surroundings, he is astonished to find small critters, beetles and bugs that he had no idea even existed. They made great models because they rarely moved, giving him a chance to set up his tripod in a manner that allowed him to get in real close to the subject.

'Hello, it's a lovely day, isn't it?' says a woman dressed in high shorts and an athletic singlet. She took him by surprise and he nearly fell over – he was crouched taking a photo, and as he stood up, he lost his footing.

'Oh, I'm sorry, I didn't mean to startle you, are you ok?' she asks.

'Yes, I am ok, I just stood up too quickly,' he replies, 'and, yes, it's a beautiful day, were you on the other side of the island?'

'Yes, I was, and it's just gorgeous. God's own backyard,' she proclaims. 'Are you going that way now?' she asks.

'Eventually. I am enjoying the rainforest at the moment. I'm hoping to get some great shots in and then I am hoping to get a great sunset,' he says.

'I was there a couple of days ago around sunset and the colours were spectacular,' she says.

'That's great. Do many people get over there at all?' he enquires.

'No, I don't think so. I've walked this track four times over the last few days and you're the first person I've seen. Though I did see a romantic couple at the far end of the beach. But other than that, it's quite secluded,' she says.

She says her goodbyes and continues on with her walk, leaving Michael to enjoy the peace and quiet. Also knowing that there is little chance of being disturbed by passers-by pleased him immensely. Not that her presence annoyed him, he was polite enough – it's just that being alone out here, he can be himself. There is no need to have a pretentious attitude, to be nice and well-liked all the time.

He continued wandering through the rainforest, discovering the smallest of tracks that snake away from the main track. Occasionally he would take a risk to see where it goes, paying no mind to the possibility of snakes. At one point, he had to jump over a fairly wide pond so that he could take some photos. With a good firm hold on all his gear, he took the leap successfully. Coming back the same way, he wasn't so lucky – he landed short and was ankle deep in murky water.

'Fuck, that was stupid,' he growls. Now with one jogger soaking wet he will have to slosh around. 'May as well make my way to the beach and hope my sock dries off in the sun.' He had packed a towel in his backpack so that if he decided to go swimming, he could do so.

The trek takes him around fifteen minutes from where he had landed in the pond. He hadn't been paying attention to the time – no wonder he is hungry, it is 12:30 p.m. As soon as he gets to the beach, he finds a log to sit on and have a few sandwiches. He washes them down with a tepid Coke and then takes his shirt off to try and get a suntan.

He falls asleep in the sun and is slightly sunburnt. What wakes him is the voice of a young woman. At first, he thinks that he is dreaming, until he sits up and grimaces. The pain in his shoulders from the sunburn is unexpected, and he knows that it is going to be worse when he gets back to his room to shower.

'I thought that you were dead, you were lying so perfectly still. I didn't mean to wake you,' says the stranger.

'Huh? No, that's ok. I'm glad you woke me up, if I'd slept any longer, my back might have blistered,' he says.

'My name is Stacy, pleased to make your acquaintance,' she says.

'Hello, I'm Michael. Are you here with your family?' he asks.

'No, I'm on my own. Oh, you mean on a holiday with my family, then, yes. I had a huge fight with my mother and went for a walk to cool off,' she says. 'I'm going in for a swim now, but glad that you're ok,' Stacy adds.

Michael watches her undress, out of her shorts and top – she already has her swimming costume on. Then with a lady like run across the sand she goes into the water with a little squeal. 'Obviously the water is cool,' he thinks and with that, he decides to go for a swim as well. He is hoping that the water would soothe the slight stinging across his shoulders.

He swims for a short while, but it is getting late in the afternoon, so he gets out, dries himself and then gets dressed. He is grateful for a warm, sunny afternoon because his pond-soaked sock is now dry. He sets up his camera gear ready for the impending sunset when Stacy also gets out. Through the corner of his eye, so as not to make it obvious, he watches her dry off and then lay on her towel. It is still quite warm and with the little sun that is left, he guesses that she is going to get as much from it as she can.

While he waits for the sun to set at a particular position on the horizon, he looks up and down the beach for any other people in the area. He notices that he and Stacy are the only people there. After about five minutes, he can see that the sun is getting close to the point he wants, and begins taking photos. The lady who had startled him on the track was absolutely right – the colours in the sky are amazing! He moves around a few times to get different angles and to change the scenery. He sees a boat sailing past in the distance and waits for it to reach the streak of light from the sun coming across the water, and snaps off three quick shots.

It doesn't take long for the sun to set, and the light begins to fade, so he packs up his gear ready for the trek back. He was smart enough to bring a torch because the walk back should take about forty minutes, and he figures that halfway home, it will be dark. He looked across to where Stacy is laying on her towel. She has fallen asleep. 'I suppose I should wake her,' he thinks out loud, and is about to walk over to her from where his gear is.

There are some medium to large rocks around which had made it easy for him to rest his things on while taking photos, and without even thinking about it, he had picked up a rock that was a little bigger than a baseball and was tossing it up and down in his hand. He is totally unaware that he has this rock, and yet when he gets to where Stacy is laying, he just stands there and watches her for some time, almost like he is in a trance – when he suddenly, without explanation, kneels down and proceeds to bash her skull in with the rock, hitting her over twenty times until he is exhausted. He didn't bring his cigarettes with him as he had been trying to give the filthy habit up, besides it costing him a fortune. Though how badly he could do with one right now.

Stacy had no idea what hit her, she had been sound asleep when she was attacked. Michael cannot leave her here, so he has to think of where he can put her. He remembers seeing a side opening off the track, about five minutes back along the trail. It wasn't too far, and he is comfortable leaving his gear where it is and coming back for it.

With the towel wrapped around her, Michael picks her up, including all of her belongings, and puts her on his shoulder, then begins the walk to hide her body. He finds an ideal place – a large tree had fallen a long time ago and had created a little cave because of the shape of the land. So, he tucks her neatly into the crevice along with all of her belongings. Being careful not to disturb the natural look of the area, he gathers as many shrubs and twigs as he could, to cover the area and try to make it look like a natural scene.

After he has done the necessary decoration with the flora, he walks back to the very narrow track that fed off the main one, and turns to look back, to make certain that if anyone comes looking, they'd surely not notice anything out of the ordinary.

Satisfied with himself, he then goes back to the beach where he makes sure that there is no trace of Stacy ever being there, covering the blood-stained sand by burying it under more sand – the deeper, the better.

Having completed the clean-up, he takes one more look around, and then picks up his belongings and heads back to his hut. With his torch to guide the way, he slowly makes his way back trying to avoid tripping. With his safe return around 7:00 p.m., Louise asks how his day went.

'It was really good. I am glad I went, now. I got some great photos. I'll upload them on the laptop after breakfast tomorrow and you can let me know which ones you like,' he says.

7

THE SEARCH

Michael is woken up early by ramblings and chatter outside, he was hoping to get a sleep-in. Fat chance of that with all that racket, and so, he gets out of bed and puts some shorts and a singlet on, and goes outside to see what the fuss was all about.

'What's going on?' Michael asks.

'My daughter didn't come home last night. She had a fight with her mother yesterday afternoon and went for a walk. She hasn't been seen since,' says Andrew Hepworth.

'Oh, I'm sorry to hear that. Have you alerted the front desk?' Michael asks Andrew.

'Yes, and they are going to organise a search party after lunch. They said to give her until then; she may have stayed with someone and is sleeping in,' says Andrew.

'That makes sense. My name is Michael and my family and I are staying in that hut just over there, number twenty-one. If you need any help, I don't have that much planned, but I'd be happy to help. I have two daughters and would hate for them not to come home,' says Michael.

'Thanks, that means a lot. I'm just so worried, as it's not like her to go off like that,' Andrew says.

'I'm sure she is ok. What was your daughter's name, in case I hear someone mentioning it,' asks Michael.

'Stacy. God, I hope she is ok,' says Andrew.

'I'm sure she is,' with that said, Michael turns around and goes inside to make a coffee.

'Good morning, Bub,' Michael says to his wife. 'I was just outside talking with a guy who says his daughter is missing. It's a horrible thought, not knowing where your child might be.'

'When did he realise that his daughter was missing?' Louise asks.

'She went off yesterday afternoon after a fight with her mother and never returned. He woke this morning to discover that her bed was still made and empty,' he says.

'Has anyone started looking for her?' she asks.

'Management is going to organise a search party after lunch, I thought that I might join them and help out. I'd be devastated if one of our girls went missing,' says Michael.

'That's a great idea. Gee, I hope that she is ok. I will watch the girls while you're out. They're too young to be involved in a search party,' Louise says.

The girls wake up around ten that morning and miss the fracas outside, and therefore have no idea about the missing girl. Their father made bacon and eggs for their breakfast, along with freshly squeezed orange juice that he purchased at the small convenience store beside the main office.

'I will be busy today and you girls will spend the day with your mum,' Michael says.

'What are you doing that takes you away from the family? You were gone most of the day yesterday. I thought this was supposed to be a family holiday,' cries Michelle.

'Look, I wasn't going to say too much but a girl appears to have gone missing, and I have volunteered to help look,' he says. 'I don't want you girls getting involved with this. I'd hate for something to go wrong while we are all separated and looking for her, I would feel better if you were with mum,' he explains.

'Ok, Dad, I totally understand. What was the girl's name?' Michelle asks.

'Her name is Stacy, but I don't know how old she is,' he says.

'If it's who I think it is, she is nineteen, she would be Wayne's sister. You know, the guy I was playing tennis with the other day,' Michelle says.

'Oh? I didn't know he had a sister. I hope the family is ok. I will keep you posted if I hear anything, ok, sweetie?' he says.

'Ok, Dad. Just be careful, ok?' she asks.

After lunch, Michael goes to the main office to make enquiries about the missing girl.

'Hi there, I'm Michael from Hut twenty-one. I heard that someone is organising a search party for a missing girl. Has she returned yet?'

The receptionist replies saying that the girl hasn't returned yet and the manager is asking for help from the guests, so if he'd like to help, she could let him know. 'I believe that he wants to get a number of people gathered on the tennis courts to discuss the necessary actions, so if you want to hang around the courts about 1:00 p.m., I'm sure you'll be able to help,' she says.

A small crowd has gathered at the tennis court, and the manager has just arrived. 'Good afternoon, everyone. I'm Richard Craymore, the manager of the resort. It came to my attention this morning that a young lady has gone missing. We waited for a short time to allow her to turn up. I am hoping that she went walking along a track and got herself lost. I have printed detailed maps of the island, and I am going to select two teams. Please come up to the table and get a map each,' Richard says.

Michael teamed up with a guy three huts down, called Simon Jones, who was a business executive for a metal fabrication company in Perth. He was taking time out from a very busy schedule to unwind as the building industry had been quite busy of late. Admittedly there wasn't much conversation between the two guys as they were mostly calling out to Stacy. Before they all headed off to the search, Michael had suggested that he and Simon look on the western track that leads to the other side of the island, as he had done that walk the other day. It was agreed, mostly with the other volunteers not being familiar with that track.

On the western track, Michael makes sure that he looks in the proximity of where he had hidden the body and suggests Simon look in the area opposite to where he is. 'Nothing over here but fallen foliage and a few small branches,' Michael says.

'Same over here,' replies Simon.

'STACY!' they yell at the same time, only to hear nothing but the wind in the trees and the birds singing their songs. When they get to the beach, they separate and agree to walk for five minutes in opposite directions, then turn around and come back. The beach is completely empty, with absolutely no sign of anyone being there over the last few days, except for a towel left near some weeds and low-lying trees.

'Hey Simon, I found a towel over here,' Michael says, as he sees Simon coming back to where they had separated.

Simon comes running for the last five or so metres and looks at it with a feeling of dismay. 'Suppose it is hers? Where are the rest of her things?' he asks.

They look at each other with a look of despair. Michael picks up the towel and says, 'She could have been swimming and drowned, but I hope not.'

'It doesn't make sense because there are no clothes or a bag,' says Simon.

'That's true, perhaps she walked here already dressed in swimmers, and she may not have needed a bag being so close to her hut,' replies Michael.

'Good point, mate. We should start heading back as I don't see anything else around,' says Simon.

They return along the same track calling her name out as often as possible, in fact, Michael thought he was losing his voice at one stage.

'STACY!' and still no answer.

'Hey, what's this?' Simon enquires.

'It looks like a lipstick,' Michael replies.

'It could be hers, but I don't see a bag or anything else around,' says Simon.

'We'll bring it back with us and hopefully someone can identify it as belonging to her,' Michael says.

Having done a thorough search of all the known tracks, there was no trace of Stacy to be found. It was decided that the authorities would be called to make an official report, and to have the police take over the search.

'Did anyone find any sign of her at all,' asked Richard. Simon said that they found a lipstick but there was no other indication that she was there at all.

'Also, we found this towel near some shrubs that could have been blown by the wind,' said Michael. 'We can't rule out that she might have been swimming and drowned,' he finished.

Stacy's mum came over quietly sobbing and had a look at the lipstick, but it wasn't a colour Stacy would have worn. Though as soon as she saw the towel, she burst into howling tears, 'NO! NO! NO! Not my baby,' she cried. Her husband grabbed a hold of her just before she collapsed to her knees.

Everyone felt a sense of uselessness and sadness. Forty people all together, including the resort staff, and the silence was deafening.

'I want to thank you all for your help today,' Andrew said, almost at a whisper. 'I won't give up looking for my daughter, I know she is alive and probably so scared.'

Richard asked the gathered crowd for their attention, 'Firstly, on behalf of Mr and Mrs Hepworth, I want to thank you all for your time and effort today. Unfortunately, we had no luck in finding Stacy, though we won't stop our search. As soon as I get back to my office, I will be calling the police on the mainland and reporting this. We can resume our search again tomorrow morning with those who can be available. I'd like to meet here again at 10:00 a.m. after a good breakfast. We'll need the energy.'

'Thanks, Richard. We appreciate all your help,' said Andrew.

'I think we should call it a day as the light will soon be gone. I'd like to suggest that we enjoy a good meal, on the house, and then a good night's rest,' says Richard. Most were verbally grateful for the free meal but the tension was thicker than a mid-winter fog.

'It's so sad about that missing girl,' someone said as the group departed quietly. Michael was quietly chuffed at how well the search went but kept a melancholy look on his face.

When he arrives back at the hut, he fills his family in on the day's events, including the towel that was found.

'Dad can I go see Wayne to comfort him?' asks Michelle.

'Not tonight, Sweetie, I think we should let the family have this time to themselves. I think it's the least that we can do. You can see him tomorrow after breakfast,' he says.

'Ok, Daddy, I think that's a good idea. And I will keep my phone with me too in case you need me,' she replies.

'Thanks, Michelle. Now the manager has awarded everyone with dinner on the house, so I think we should get changed and go eat, I'm starving,' he says.

Though the restaurant was packed to capacity that night, and you would expect it to be extremely noisy, it was so quiet that you could hear the banging and clanging coming from the kitchen. The only other predominant noise that could be heard was the occasional sobbing and sniffling from a few patrons. Hardly a word was spoken – naturally, nobody knew what to say.

Two days later, the Huberts left to go home, along with three other families. Stacy was still missing, and the Hepworths extended their stay on the island in the hope that the police would find something. God knows they were going over the island with a fine-toothed comb.

8

ROUTINE

The flight home is rather quiet and dull. The atmosphere on board the plane is a sombre one. The experience on the island has left them all feeling saddened. Danielle and Michelle are quietly chatting with each about their holiday and basically keeping to themselves. They are not concerned with window seats this time; they just want to get home and get back to their routine.

'Don't tell dad but I got Wayne's mobile phone number so I can keep in touch with him,' says Michelle.

'I won't but wouldn't dad be cranky if he found out?' Danielle says.

'Yeah, he would be, and when I am ready I will tell him, but right now it's just too soon,' she replies.

'I found out that he lives in Sydney too, he like lives in Chatswood and is in year twelve. When things cool down, he wants to meet up,' says Michelle.

'I don't think dad will be happy with that, Sis, but I won't say anything,' says Danielle.

'Thanks, Danni, you're the best,' Michelle says.

'Are you going to stay in touch with the Hepworths, Michael?' asks Louise.

'No, I don't think so. It's sad what happened, but there's nothing more I can do,' he says.

'I was kind of hoping to stay in touch myself, I feel so sorry for them,' she says.

'Well if it's what you want to do, I'm sure that they will appreciate the support,' he says. Louise can't help but think that Michael seems a little cold towards the situation, maybe it's just his way of dealing with it, she thinks.

The plane landed at Sydney Domestic on time and after waiting ten minutes to collect their bags, they slowly make their way back to the car.

'I just have to pay for the parking and we can go. Does anyone want to stop at Macca's for lunch?' asks Michael. None of them are particularly hungry but all agree that a lunch stop was a good idea. Michael is in an unusually flat mood and sensibly the family choose not to question it. After all, it wasn't the holiday that any of them dreamt of.

On the way home, Michael diverts their trip by stopping to get the *Sunday Telegraph*, not something that he does often, but it will settle him when he gets home. When they pulled up in the driveway, everyone lets out a sigh, almost all at the same time.

'It has never felt so good to be home,' Louise says.

'I know, huh. I am going straight to my room to read,' says Danielle. Yes, Danielle is a bit of a bookworm like her mum.

'Yeah, I'm gonna veg out on the lounge with my iPad,' says Michelle.

'Only after we have all finished unpacking – dirty clothes in the laundry basket as well, please,' says Michael.

After everyone unpacks all of their things, Louise gets straight into clothes washing while the girls do their thing. Meanwhile, Michael goes out to the back veranda to read the paper and grabs a beer from the fridge. The usual hogwash stories in the paper; more political fighting in Canberra. Another National Rugby League (NRL) player charged with offensive behaviour in a city bar. A drive-by shooting in Lakemba.

He is surprised that there is no article on the disappearance of the girl on Whitsunday Island, or on the case that the police questioned him about. He reads the comics – he's a big fan of Garfield and Snake Tales – then sits and does the crossword.

After a few beers, he goes to shower and then comes down to help Louise prepare dinner. At the dinner table, there is some light talk about the upcoming week at school and work. Michelle's project in science is due Wednesday and she is only halfway through making a volcano. Danielle has nothing due but is looking forward to seeing her friends again. Louise is on call with her temp agency so has little planned, and Michael, as far as he knows, until he gets to work, has the usual local deliveries.

Monday morning comes too quickly and Michael really isn't in the mood today. His demons are surfacing and angry. He slowly drives into the car park at work and sits in his car for five minutes to compose himself. He gets the courage to get out and face the day, puts on his happy face and strolls into Jordan's office.

'Good morning, Mike. How was your holiday?' asks Jordan.

'G'day, Jords, it was amazing. I am so relaxed. Pity, it wasn't longer,' he says.

'Yeah, know that feeling. You always need a holiday to get over your holiday,' Jordan says, and they both laugh heartedly.

'Ok, so what have you got for me today,' asks Michael.

'A few drops out in Windsor, then to Ingleburn,' says Jordan.

'Sweet, I'll get the truck and start getting ready,' Michael replies.

'No probs, Mike,' Jordan says.

After getting on the road, he calls Louise just to make sure that she is ok. She is so glad that he called because strangely the house feels too big and by eight in the morning she had been on to her second glass of white wine. She usually doesn't drink so early, but for some reason she feels unstable.

'Maybe the holiday had more of an effect on me,' she tells him.

'I understand, Bub, just go easy, ok?' he says.

She agreed with herself to make that the last glass, however, she ended up finishing the bottle. A trend that slowly takes hold, and a secret she keeps for a long time.

So, life goes back to a relatively normal routine, except that all four of them have been changed forever by their holiday on Whitsunday Island. Michelle becomes more withdrawn from the family and her mum doesn't really notice. She just thinks that it's a typical moody teenager thing. Poor Danielle feels left out as the family becomes despondent, so she starts turning to punk music and black clothes. She starts wearing heavy make-up at the age of thirteen and is disobedient at school. The teachers have tried consoling her with no great success. She seems to have her father's trait of making others believe that everything is fine. Three days later, Danielle is caught shoplifting junk jewellery and is let off with a warning. She doesn't tell her parents about it, which is until she is caught six months later stealing electronic goods. Michelle's situation really upsets her father, as she starts to see Wayne after school. A connection with his past is something that he doesn't want. So, they all have their own thing happening and are somehow managing to continue daily life without anyone else recognising any issues. Caught up in their own demons – that somehow consume them – without any of them realising this fact.

The only person to recognise that something is a little different is Michael. Louise seems to think that she has her drinking well hidden. It's a little hard not to notice that there are several empty wine bottles in the recycling bin at the end of each week, considering that he takes the bins out each Tuesday night. As much as he loves and adores his wife, he has no idea how to help her; how to comfort her. So, instead, he lets her continue her drinking. After all, the house is kept clean and tidy. It's not hurting anyone, and besides, he has done far worse, so who is he to criticise.

Life rolls along at a slow and steady pace with no particular event to rattle the barn door. Though the girls are becoming rebellious, they manage to get really good grades in school, and with Michelle being in year ten, she is starting to study hard for future exams. She has plans for a university course in Medicine. She hasn't yet decided on any specific field, but she feels that forensic science might be really interesting.

If only her father knew – the irony of a serial killer and a forensics daughter.

Louise keeps up her bookkeeping work with the Temp agency and manages to get a better hold of her drinking. She could feel that she was losing control of her life and that it would start affecting the family. Michael notices that there are less bottles in the recycling bin each week and is happy.

A few weeks after the Huberts returned from their disturbing holiday, Michael is asked to do a very important delivery.

'Mike, I want to know if you are interested in doing an interstate trip for me,' asks Jordan.

'Sure, I'll ask my family about it just to make sure that they are okay with me being gone a couple of days. Where is it to?' he asks.

'Adelaide, and you will probably be gone a week. This is an important client and they are happy to pay the expenses. I know you are capable of this trip, and frankly I'd prefer that you do this job,' Jordan said.

Michael gets home at a reasonable hour and everything seems ok, even the girls are getting along. Just recently they had been getting on each other's nerves so it was nice to see them getting along for a change.

'I need to ask you all a question,' says Michael. 'Danielle are you listening or just playing with your iPad? Put it down. I've told you before I don't want it at the dinner table. Work wants me to do a trip to Adelaide next week and I'll be gone the whole week. Is everyone ok with this?' he asks.

There is a moment of silence as they all absorb this information, which strangely feels like minutes instead of seconds.

'That's cool, Daddy, I don't have my school play for a couple of weeks yet,' says Danni.

'Ok, thanks, guys, I'll let my boss know in the morning,' he says.

So, the trip gets planned and Michael is actually looking forward to getting away for a while.

9

MURDER MYSTERY

- - - - - - -

With four victims already, Michael has come to enjoy the thrill of the chase. To catch his victim unawares and strike hard. This particular murder will not be discovered for many years to come.

A serial killer usually has a method of operation or an MO. While this is true with Michael, for him it is the way he kills his victim, and rarely does he sway from this method. However, he likes to mix it up with where he leaves his victims, and it will usually be determined by the landscape and the conditions of the area at the time.

The only time that Michael finds to fulfil this horrid affliction is when he is on a long drive. This time is no different. A trip to the Riverina area of NSW was meant to be a return trip that day. His delivery was to a farm property in Leeton where a client was building a small guest house for families to stay when they visited.

The reason for the delay was that the farmer had organised a small crane truck to unload the timber, but it broke down on the way from the yard. The parts that were required had to come from West Wyalong, about an hour or so north. Then, of course, they tried to get a diesel mechanic out when the parts finally arrived. He rang Jordan to inform him of the situation, everything was ok.

'Yeah, well I will rearrange the deliveries that you had scheduled. Just keep receipts for everything so that when you get back, we can determine what the company will cover you for. Accommodation is a definite, and if you need to hire a car for the day, keep the receipt as well. Just keep me in the loop, ok, Mike?' says Jordan.

So, Michael gets a lift into town and there he finds a pub that has a room for the night. It was around four in the afternoon when Michael gets dropped off at the pub. After he pays cash for the room, he goes for a stroll. He wishes that he had his camera with him as the buildings are so grand and beautiful. Some look like they have frozen in time from the eighteenth century; their condition is amazing.

Now he decides to do something quite out of his comfort zone and walks into an antiques store. Nothing really catches his eye, but he had only been thinking of buying a trinket for his wife.

'Excuse me, miss, how much are you asking for this thing in the cabinet,' he enquires.

'You mean the 1934 pewter jewellery box? I am asking $450. Is it for someone special?' Maureen asks.

'Yes, it's for my wife. It's our twentieth wedding anniversary soon, and I figured I had better find something while I am thinking about it. You know what us blokes are like. Lucky to remember at all,' he says.

'Yes, I know only too well what men are like. My husband, god bless his soul, he was a shocker. He'd sometimes forget his own birthday. He's been gone now for four and a half years,' she says.

'Oh, I'm sorry to hear that. If you don't mind me asking, what did he die from?' he asks.

'That's ok, it was lung cancer. He was a heavy smoker – a two-pack-a-day smoker up to the day he died. Even though he knew he was dying he wouldn't give them up. Stubborn old mule he was. But I loved that man with all of my heart,' she sighs.

'Because you are so kind to remember your anniversary I'll accept $400, even,' she says.

'Well that is so kind of you. I'll take it, and, thank you. I am sorry for your loss too. I'd be devastated if I lost my wife,' he says.

'Don't be sorry. He had a good life,' she replies.

'If it's ok with you I'd like to wander around town for a little while and then come and get the jewellery box. I am staying for the day as the delivery I was making got held back coz of mechanical problems,' he says.

'Feel free, and if you need me, just holler, name's Maureen,' she says.

'Thanks, pleased to meet you. I'm Michael,' he replies.

After browsing for roughly ten minutes, Michael leaves to visit some other stores. Finding nothing of interest, he goes back to the antiques store and collects his item, says a polite goodbye and leaves. He wanders around town for a little longer, keeping to himself, until a little after six and then goes back to his room. He had bought a few toiletries and a change of clothes, all with cash, so he could freshen up for tea.

After a long hot shower, he goes downstairs and orders something for dinner. 'G'day, I'll have the schnitzel parmigiana with veggies, please,' he says.

'Table fourteen and we'll bring it out to you,' says the lady at the register. She is as rough as a junkyard pit bull, but he doesn't care. He would prefer to just get a decent feed, a few beers and relax. He is in no mood to make small talk with someone who looks like they'd rip his throat out for shits and giggles.

After his third beer – the pit bull had cleared his table – a band is in the middle of setting up. He wonders what kind of music they will play. Had he looked around the pub a little better he would have noticed posters advertising tonight's band. The Axles starting at 7:00 p.m. 'Covering classic Aussie rock songs,' the poster has written on it. 'This could be interesting,' he thinks to himself. So, he stays. He watches as the crowd grows in numbers and isn't surprised at the number of young people there. He gets up and goes to the bar just as the band starts playing, so, he has to yell in order to get another beer.

A woman who looks about nineteen is standing beside him and has a cheeky grin on her face. 'Not used to the noise, huh,' she says.

'Yeah, usually. They took me by surprise. Whatcha drinkin'?' he asks. He sees this asan opportunity for a free drink.

'Vodka and orange,' she says.

'And a vodka with OJ, please,' he tells the barman. 'Name's Michael, pleased to meet you.' He extends his hand.

'Hi, I'm Monica. Thanks for the drink,' she says.

'No probs, can I ask you for a dance later?' he says.

'Sure, old man, but I'll come and get you,' she says. 'Oh, and thanks again for the drink,' she says as she walked away.

It is about forty minutes and two more beers later that she comes over to see if he still wants the dance. Mind you, he has no clue how to dance but he is enjoying the music. They dance for about an hour, on and off, when Monica says that she has to get going as she has an early start the next day. 'I'll call for a taxi, thanks again for the drinks and dance,' she says.

'Don't be silly. I'm staying here at the pub and I am happy to drive you home, save your money. I insist,' he says. After what felt like minutes of her looking him up and down and checking him over, she finally agrees.

'I am parked in the back car park so you can start walking. I'll race upstairs and grab my keys. I don't have them on me coz I wasn't expecting to go anywhere tonight,' he says.

So, off she goes without saying goodbye to any of her friends. It completely slips her mind. Michael fumbled around in his room, finds his keys and grabs a jacket off his bed. He walks past the cleaner's room, marked as so, and puts his ear against the door to listen. Nobody is home and he discovers that the door isn't locked either. So, he goes in and has a quick look around. He finds what he is looking for and puts it in the inside pocket of his jacket and then leaves, closing the door behind him.

'Sorry that took so long, I had to pee and then couldn't find my keys. This is the car, Mavis Rental, it's not a bad little car either,' he explains as he opens the passenger side door for her.

'Wow nobody's done that before,' she says.

'What? Open your door?' he says.

'Yes, that's so old school I didn't think anyone did that anymore,' she says.

'Yeah, I guess it is old school. It's just the way I was brought up,' he says.

'So how far do you live?' Michael asks.

'Oh, it's about thirty minutes from here,' says Monica.

'That would have cost a bit in the taxi, wouldn't it?' he asks.

'Oh, about forty bucks, but I budget for that when I want to go out,' she replies.

'Well, that's ok, then. So, what do you do, are you working?' he asks.

'Yes, I am working. I am training to be a legal secretary. I then want to go to university to be a criminal lawyer,' she explains.

'Where would you go to uni?' he asks.

'I would like to go to Monash University in Victoria. Of course, I would apply to live on campus if I could, or maybe find shared accommodation, but that's not for a few years yet,' she says. 'So, what you do? I'm guessing that you don't live locally,' she asks.

'I'm a truck driver from Sydney. I had a large delivery for a farm here. A crane was supposed to be there to unload the truck but it broke down and they have to wait for parts. So, until it's fixed, I am stuck here,' he says.

'Oh, sorry, I meant to tell you to turn right just back there,' said Monica.

'That's ok, I will do a U-turn just up the road,' he says.

As Michael drove into Leeton, he has seen a sign for a small, abandoned mine shaft with a 'Warning. Keep Out. Danger. Abandoned mine shaft board' hanging off a fence on a side road. With little to do but enjoy the view while driving, this sign had caught his eye, and for him it had been something that he had wanted to remember.

'That's interesting. Must have been from the gold mining era of the1800s. I would have thought that they'd have filled it in,' he says out loud while driving past it again now.

Monica is beginning to suddenly feel uncomfortable because Michael is not showing any signs of slowing down to turn around.

Michael plays around with the accelerator pedal, to make it appear that he is out of fuel, and then turns the engine off. He lets the car roll to a stop when he says, 'Bugger, I swear I had more fuel than that. The gauge says we have plenty of fuel; it might be a clogged fuel line. I'll get out and have a look.'

So, he pops open the bonnet and gets out. He fumbles around as if he is actually fixing the problem when Monica gets out to have a cigarette. 'Do you think this will take long?' she asks.

'No, not long at all, I'll have this problem fixed real soon,' he says. He didn't have to wait long before she turns her back to him – when he suddenly pulls a hammer from inside of his jacket and bashes her skull in. He loses count of the number of times he hits her and doesn't care.

He collects her purse from the front seat and puts it in the back pocket of his jeans, and then goes to where she fell. He picks her up and carries her for almost a kilometre to the mineshaft. His only challenge is to hoist his legs over the loose wired fence without tearing his clothes. He cannot afford to leave any evidence whatsoever. This is a perimeter fence meant to keep people out. With that done, he walks a distance of about three hundred more metres from the fence to where the shaft is. He has to put her down because it is covered. Not greatly though, as he manages quite easily to move without disturbing the area. He then picks up the body, gently sits her on the edge and gives her a push, then throws her purse in afterwards. It is very deep because it takes a little while before he hears the thud and the crack of breaking bones. Satisfied with his task, he places the cover back in its place, making sure to check that it looks like it hasn't been touched, and then he leaves.

Back at the pub, he decides to have one more beer, a 'well done, champ' beer to celebrate. After that it is time for bed. The next morning, he wakes up feeling a little seedy, but he did drink more than he usually remwould, so he figures that it is to be expected.

Around 11:35 a.m., he receives a phone call to say that the crane was fixed and on its way. 'Thanks, can someone come out and get me? Say around midday?' he asks.

'Yeah, mate, I'll send Smiffy,' was the reply.

Back at the farm, and the truck had already been unloaded, so he gets the paperwork signed, then phones Jordan. 'Hi, Jords, the truck just got unloaded so I'm heading straight back. If I get good traffic I hope to get back by five maybe six at the latest.'

'That's cool, just drive safely. See ya when you get back,' Jordan said.

Back on the road, and he is going over last night in his mind. 'They will NEVER find this one. Or would they?'

10

ON THE ROAD

Michael woke very early Wednesday morning to get to work before 5:00 a.m., so that he could get out of Sydney before the morning peak-hour traffic became a bottleneck car park. Jordan had a spare key cut for him so that he could get access to the yard, pick up the truck and lock the gate behind him.

'Mornin, mate,' Michael says to the security guard who is doing a routine patrol of the premises.

'Morning, you must be Michael. I was told that you would be here around this time. Where are you headed?' asks the security guard.

'I'm headed for Adelaide, a suburb called Kilburn. Never heard of it though,' Michael says. 'Thank god for satellite navigation now as I hate carrying around a half a dozen street directories.'

'Well good luck to ya, mate, have a great time and drive safely. You know what that Hume Highway can be like,' the security guard says.

'Yeah, I remember that bus and semi-trailer accident about nine months ago. Tragic accident too, fourteen people died coz the truck driver fell asleep at the wheel,' says Michael.

Michael lights up a cigarette – still can't give up this disgusting habit – unlocks the gate and closes it behind him. Because of the long trip, he goes over the truck thoroughly, checking the oil and water. He starts the truck first and lets it idle so that he can build the air pressure required for the brakes. He walks around the truck, kicking the tyres with his steel capped boots to check for any flats. He goes back to the cabin and switches all of the truck lights on, then does another walk around to make sure that no globes have blown. One final check is required and probably the most important one of all, that the load is in the correctly loaded position and tightly secured. With the dog and chains in place, he uses a long steel pipe and bangs on the chains to check the tension.

Now that he is completely satisfied with everything, he leaves the truck idling and goes into the lunchroom to make a coffee to-go in his thermos travel mug. He takes the coffee outside, leans against the front of the truck and sips it while watching the colours in the sky slowly change from black to purple, as the sun starts to peek one eye over the horizon. 'Enough fucking around, pal,' he mumbles, as he flicks the spent cigarette to the ground and turns to climb up into the driver's seat. He drives slowly and steadily until he gets far enough out from the yard, then he locks the gate, is moving. As expected, there is light traffic all the way to the Campbelltown on-ramp to the freeway. Smooth sailing for a few hours.

After a faultless drive, it is time to pull over and Sutton Forest is an ideal place. It consists of a petrol/convenience station, truck stop, roadside restaurant and McDonalds, plus toilets and amenities. A good high-cholesterol fed breakfast sounded good so after parking the truck and locking it he heads for the restaurant. 'Good morning, sweetheart, how goes it?' Michael says in a real chipper voice.

'Good morning, stranger, what'll it be this morning?' the waitress asks.

'Hmmm, I will get the Truck Load Hamburger with fries and a large black coffee, no sugar please.'

He pays for his breakfast and takes a number to a booth by the window at the far end of the restaurant. On his way, he grabs the stamped daily newspaper from a rack near the counter and begins to peruse, flicking through to the comic page. On that same page there is a crossword puzzle that someone else has started, so he takes his pen from his shirt pocket and continues with the puzzle. 'Ok, six-letter word for 'fine rain falling after sunset,' he thinks out loud. He remembers seeing this word recently in a newspaper weather report. 'Third letter R,' he says. Just as he is about to remember the word, a waitress brings his coffee over with a complimentary cookie. 'Thanks, darlin',' he says as she walks away.

'Serein, that's it,' he says, and quickly writes it in seven down. He remarks at the speed of the service when a waitress brings his breakfast over. 'Thanks, love, service is pretty quick, I must say.'

'Oh, we have to be with the hundreds that we get walking through the door,' she says. This suits him fine because he can't afford to hang around for too long. There is nothing in the paper that fascinates him so he folds it and puts it aside while he finishes his breakfast. His OCD kicks in, and he takes his mug, plate and cutlery to the counter and thanks them for a great brekkie. Before he leaves, though, he goes to the convenience store to grab a drink and a chocolate bar for the road.

Firstly, before he gets back into his truck he does another check to ensure that the load hasn't become loose and has shifted. He picks up the steel pipe and gives the chains a bang. Luckily for him that he did as one of the chains had become sloppy, so he tightens it, then puts the pipe back on the truck's tray.

Next stop, Mildura.

Approximately forty-five kilometres of being back on the road, there is a random roadside check of all trucks. The Department of Roads and Transport or the DRT have set up an area where trucks are able to pull over without disrupting the highway traffic. Michael is flagged to pull over, which he does without hesitation.

'Hello there, can I see your papers please,' asks the inspector. At first, he had no idea what the inspector meant – what papers – then he realises that the inspector wants to see the delivery docket for the load.

'Yeah, give me a sec, they fell on the floor a little way back,' Michael says. After he takes his sweet time picking up the papers – after all, he has to take his seat belt off – he hands them to the inspector with a friendly smile.

'Thanks, please stay in your truck while I go through your papers. I will then be looking over your truck,' says the inspector. Knowing that he was going to be there for a while, he decides to phone Jordan to let him know what's going on.

'Good afternoon, KRT, this is Jordan.'

'Yeah, hi Jords, it's Mike. I have just been pulled over by the DRT for a random truck check. I could be here for a while, so I just wanted to touch base. Is there anything I should be worried about?' he asks.

'No, Mike, it's all legit. We made sure that your load was within the GVM (Gross Vehicle Mass) limits, and remember, we put new tyres on it six months ago,' Jordan says.

'Ok, thanks, and yeah I wasn't worried about the tyres, just the load,' Michael says, sounding annoyed. He was there when the tyres were fitted – it took over four hours to fit and balance, a day wasted in his opinion – so, when Jordan reminds him, he is annoyed that Jordan had forgotten. Forget the fact that Jordan has a lot to deal with, the fact that his tone of voice was so blasé is what annoys him.

The inspector finally came back to him after making him wait twenty-three minutes. Yes, Michael was timing it to put it in his logbook. 'Everything is in order. I just need you to drive over onto the weight bridge, and we are done,' says the inspector. This whole process is becoming boring and tedious, yet begrudgingly, he does as he is instructed. Thankfully, it only takes a couple of minutes to get the truck weighed and the information recorded, and then he is free to get back on the road.

A thunderstorm is brewing in the distance and this is probably his greatest fear. The lightening is an array of streaks in the darkening clouds, creating an ominous atmosphere, one in which his anxiety would make the drive quite challenging.

Last year, without the company's knowledge, he installed a very expensive stereo system with solid bass speakers of two hundred watts, as he has a thing for quality sound. If and when he leaves his job, he intends to have the old stereo system put back in. Most days he is happy to listen to talk-back radio, but there are days when they just crap on. Thankfully, he also carries burnt copies of his favourite CDs, and this is the ideal time to grab one out and crank it hard.

He acts quickly as the thunder starts becoming frequent, so he reaches for his CD folder and flicks it open with his left hand and grabs the first disc that the folder opens to. He blindly selects The Angels' 'No Exit' album, an old favourite. He pops the CD in, cranks the volume and starts singing at the top of his lungs, reminiscing the time when he saw The Angels live at The Horden Pavilion, right up against the stage. It is time to change the gear and slow the truck down as the rain is becoming very heavy—'Waiting for Mr. Damage,' he bellows. He is suddenly puzzled, almost certain that he can see someone walking along the road waving him down. He lowers the volume and slows down a little more. Luckily for the person walking, Michael was driving slower than usual and was able to stop. 'Jump in, quick,' Michael says.

'Thanks, man, I owe you one. My car broke down about a kilometre back and I don't have any cash for a tow truck. Man, is it pissing down out there or what?' the hiker says.

'Yeah, I haven't seen it this heavy in a while. End of summer storm, I guess,' Michael says.

'So, where are you headed?' asks Michael.

'The next town is Narrandera, so, if that's ok with you, I can jump out there,' says the wet and weary hiker.

'Yeah, sure, that's cool. Name's Michael by the way.'

'Adrian Jackson, pleased to meet you,' the hiker says. 'So, where you going, Michael?'

'Adelaide, a little behind schedule too, but I can make the time up. I am staying overnight in Mildura so I'll get an early start tomorrow,' says Michael.

Michael is glad to have the company as he can talk and be distracted from the storm. They chat lightly about 'man things' like fishing. Adrian is rebuilding a replica GTHO for the Summer Nats next year.

'You know, I've never been to the Nats,' says Michael.

'Seriously? Man, you'd love it. Hot cars burning shit loads of rubber. Hot girls in next to nothing. It's a great weekend,' says Adrian.

'Might try and get there next year, it's in January, isn't it?' Michael asks.

'Too right, mate. Next year is the twenty-fifth year, so I reckon it's gonna be huge. You should try and get down there,' Adrian says.

A short while later they arrive in Narrandera where it hasn't rained at all. Michael drops him outside the town pub and says his goodbye.

'Thanks again, mate. Hope to see you next year, huh,' Adrian says, as he steps out of the truck.

'You're welcome, and who knows. See ya,' Michael says. Only a few hours to Mildura where he'll stop for the day.

Safely arriving at Mildura at around seven that evening, the usual road trip routine occurs – completing the truck logbook, checking into a room, showering, having a meal and then back to the room for an early night. The next day he checks out and is back on the road by 6:00 a.m. with a quick breakfast stop at McDonalds. From there it is non-stop to Adelaide and then to Kilburn. Two days to get to Adelaide is as he had expected, and he was happy to take a break from driving. If he can have his truck unloaded by one in the afternoon, he can be back in Mildura in time for dinner. Another sleep over there and then back home.

Meanwhile, there is a small backlog of deliveries and he is third in line. 'Reliability, it isn't too much to ask for,' he mutters under his breath. 'You'd think that they would organise their delivery schedule better,' he continues. So, while he waits, he fills out his logbook, which only takes about five minutes to complete. About twenty minutes later, he is getting unloaded, after which he gets the necessary paperwork signed and quickly tidies the tray of the truck, and then he heads out to find somewhere that he can park the truck without getting a parking ticket. But, before he can go and find somewhere to get lunch, he is told that he has to take a load of timber back with him, as Jordan had phoned ahead to approve the order.

Another warm day and with lunch out of the way, it is time to head back to the truck to make the four-hour trip back to Mildura. Now that the truck has had a while to cool down, he once again checks things over to make sure the truck is in reliable order. Back on the road with no enthusiasm at all, he feels something is lacking. There is an emptiness inside of him that he is quite familiar with, yet there is no way to fill this right now.

He needs to kill again. Can he find a way before he gets back to Sydney? He certainly hopes so. Only time will tell.

11

THE ONE THAT GOT AWAY

- - - - - - -

Mistakes happen from time to time and we usually learn from them, they are often called lessons in life. But there are some things that we simply cannot afford to make mistakes with. Michael is no exception to the rule.

Mildura is a decent-sized country town with its fair share of crime. Two nights before Michael first arrived, there was a stabbing in the town, a fight had started between two guys over a girl. When Michael returned from Kilburn and found accommodation at the same pub, a different room this time, one with a balcony, he bought a copy of the local paper up to his room along with a six-pack of beer he had acquired from the bottle shop. He knows he risks losing his licence if he is caught, as the blood alcohol level for a truck driver is zero, but today he doesn't care.

On page five, there is the article about the stabbing a few nights ago. 'A twenty-two-year-old male has been arrested over the stabbing of a nineteen-year-old male at the Commercial Union Hotel on Saturday night. The fight is rumoured to have started over an argument about a girl who was there at the scene. Statements have been taken and the case will be heard in court in the coming weeks. The nineteen-year-old remains in a stable condition at The Mildura Base Hospital,' reads the story.

'Friggen kids these days with weapons. Whatever happened to using your fists,' he says sitting on the balcony enjoying a cigarette and a cold beer. A kookaburra lands on the edge of his balcony and stares him dead in the eyes. It scares the crap outta him and he spills his beer, yelling out in surprise. The bird just sits there staring right at him. 'What the bloody hell do you want, ya little turd. I haven't got any food for you,' he says. And just like that, as if the bird knew exactly what he said, he flew off.

So, after cleaning the spill and getting another beer from the fridge, he goes back to reading the newspaper. A lot of town stuff, local sports teams getting ready for the footy season. The Mildura Ravens were semi-finalists last year and there is a lot of support from local businesses to sponsor them. He stumbles upon the crossword puzzle and relaxes with a pen in his hand. After a half hour of twisting his brain inside-out with the crossword, he gets up and changes into a more casual evening get up and then goes for a walk to see what food is on offer.

A Mexican restaurant called Casa De Banquete has a nice sound to it. He can't read Spanish and has no idea what it means, but the word 'Banquete' caught his eye, close to banquet, which means good food, and so he goes in.

'Good evening, Senor, would you like a table tonight?' asks the attendant at the front desk.

'Yes, please, just for one,' Michael replies. He is seated near the window so that he has a view of the outside world. Just a few minutes later, a young couple arrives and is seated quite close to him.

Michael orders a lemon squash to start with and then he closely studies the menu, uncertain of the choices. He decides to play it safe and goes with the nachos with a side salad. The service is slow tonight and while he is waiting for his meal, he switches from glancing at the young girl a few tables away to watching the occasional car or truck drive by outside. It's a cloudless night and the moon looks full and bright in the sky, casting shadows across the street. He doesn't realise that he is surprised to see a small group of teenage boys rolling past on skate boards, jumping off the pathway onto the road and back on. 'One day I'm going to run one of those inconsiderate jerks down. They've got absolutely no respect for their environment,' he quietly says to himself.

Slightly annoyed by the innocent boys, he glances back to the young girl who is seated in a position that allows him to look almost directly at her. Of course, the couple are aware of his presence but choose to ignore him. After all, he is a passing figure in town and they only like to mingle with the college group in town. The girl has long flowing sandy blonde hair with the most amazing electric blue eyes. Her smile lights up the whole restaurant, and momentarily Michael is caught in her aura. What snaps him out of his stare – the kind where someone would think that he is staring into nowhere – is the waiter with his meal.

'Here's your nachos, will that be all for now?' the waiter asks.

'Yes, thanks,' he replies.

Towards the end of his meal, the couple are close to finishing their meal as well. During their meal, he could hear raised voices from the table but couldn't make out what they were arguing about. Though once he thought he saw a few tears in her eyes but he kept out of their affairs. He got to thinking about his girls and the way that they have changed a little since the Whitsunday Island holiday. All of a sudden, he felt so alone, and realised just how much he missed his daughters smiles. As he finished his meal and got up to pay his bill, he walked past the couple and heard the girl say to the guy, 'I hate you, it's all your fault,' with tears in her eyes. He ignores the charade and pays for his meal and then goes outside and lights up a cigarette, 'Must get another pack in the morning,' he says.

Though it's a warm night he can feel a chill in the air, winter is on its way and it might just be a cold one this year. He stands outside a bookstore, looking in the window at the variety of used books, smoking and minding his own business, when he is disturbed by the couple who are still arguing as they walk out of the restaurant.

'Go to hell, Jason, you're nothing but a two-timing bastard. Fuck off, and don't ever call me, that slut can have you,' she screams at him. She swiftly turns around and walks off, face soaked with tears and her make-up running.

Jason gives her the finger and says, 'Fuck you, you weren't that great anyway,' as he crosses the road, to get into his Holden Ute. He leaves the area, burning rubber, and a cloud of smoke, and Michael quietly hides in the alcove of the book store, just out of sight.

He waits for about one minute before he decides to follow the girl. You know, just to make sure Jason doesn't come back to do her any harm. He is grateful for having chosen his joggers as they have a quiet sole, and she doesn't hear him follow her. She is still sobbing after her fight with her now ex-boyfriend, and is blindly walking in any direction, just clearing her head. Michael is a comfortable distance behind her and cannot hear her sobs, but he judges by the way her shoulders hitch up and down, that she was still crying and totally unaware that she has company.

They both walk north-east towards a park that leads to the Murray River, and the area is completely deserted. Suddenly Michael picks up the pace, and in seconds he is almost directly behind her, and pounces on her with a hard right-hand punch to the back of the head, knocking her to the ground, and almost knocking her unconscious. With a quick glance around him, he grabs her by the wrists and drags her into the darkness of the overhead bridge, whereupon he slams her to the ground. Satisfied that she isn't moving, he then looks around for a heavy object, and can see on the other side of the underpass that there are a few decent-sized rocks under a piece of graffiti, a second glance around and he darts across to get the rock.

While Michael is going to get his weapon of choice, the young girl sits awkwardly against the concrete wall of the underpass trying to stay very quiet. Her head is pounding and her vision is slightly blurred, but she is aware that she has been hit from behind. At first, she thinks it was Jason who had come up behind her, he is cowardly like that. She had seen him in a fight once where he sucker punched a guy in the back of the head. Almost killed the guy too, so naturally, she thought it was him, until she tried hard to focus and noticed that the figure walking away from her was too solid and tall to be Jason.

With all of her strength and stealth, she slowly stands up and sneaks around and back up to the pathway. Just as she puts a foot onto the path she hears her attacker yell out, 'Bitch, get back here. I am not finished with you yet,' and she immediately starts running as hard as she could. She runs harder than she ever had in her entire life despite the pounding in the back of her head. Several metres down the pathway and running towards the road, she can see a car coming and starts waving her hands and arms frantically, yelling for help.

Just as Michael turns around from picking up a rock, he sees his victim leaving the underpass and gives chase. He trips on a raised concrete edge, kicking his right foot almost to the point of breaking his big toe. This slows him down and he fears that she will escape from him altogether. His fears are closer than ever because as she approaches the main walkway he can see a car heading towards them, and the girl is screaming and waving her arms. He suddenly dashes to the right and hides behind a tree so that the approaching vehicle cannot see him – hopefully. He knows he has lost this victim and figures that it is safer to hide from view so that he cannot be identified, he's hoping the girl didn't get a good look at him either. He has to stay low and hidden for a good five minutes so that the girl has time to get away.

'Help me, please,' she yells as the car approaches and the driver notices her. He pulls over and she gets in, explaining that she was just attacked by a stranger. Someone that she hasn't seen before and is possibly from out of town. The driver takes her to the hospital for observation and the police are called to make a report. Meanwhile, Michael quietly makes his way back to the pub trying not to limp on his sore foot. The less that he can be noticed, the better.

He is back at the pub, and thankfully there is a side entrance door where he was able to sneak upstairs and into his room. He quickly packs all of his belongings. He takes his things to the truck that is parked a few streets away and then comes back in the same way, making his way into the pub to let the staff know that there has been an emergency at home and he has to leave early. He tips them a hundred dollars for the inconvenience, hands back the keys to his room and quickly leaves.

He is unseen from the underpass to the pub, and from there to his truck. He starts the truck and lets it idle to build up the air pressure before casually leaving town. He drives for about two hours before pulling over. He locks the doors and grabs his bag, leaning it against the passenger door, pulls his jacket over him and sleeps.

Tomorrow is another day.

12

ONE FOR THE ROAD

The Australian landscape has an amazing variety of sweeping green hills, vast open land and thick bushland, all of which can be seen driving through any state. There are numerous signs for many reasons, including 'Wildlife Ahead,' or indications of curves and bends in the road. When you cross the border into another state, there is a big welcoming sign. If you happen to miss this by being distracted, then there really is no other way to know you have changed states.

This is the case with Michael, as he is fumbling around with his CDs when he is signalled by NSW police to pull over. He immediately thinks that they are out of their jurisdiction and isn't going to pull over but realises that at one point he must have crossed the border, he knows that he was close enough. Then his heart jumps up into his throat. 'Fuck I hope this isn't about that bitch in Mildura,' he croaks, as he pulls the truck to the side of the road. As far as his logbook goes, he knows that isn't going to be an issue. He is quite anal about making sure it is filled out correctly, so he is now uncomfortable about this, the pit of his stomach starting to feel like lead.

'Hello, driver, do you know what the speed limit is for this section of road?' asks the officer. Michael hadn't noticed that the speed limit had dropped from 100 to 80 km/h and was still comfortably cruising along listening to Transvision Vamp when he wanted a change. Van Halen's 5150 album would do just nicely. Whoop! Whoop! The sound of the police siren changed all that.

'Yeah, it's a hundred,' says Michael.

'Wrong. Six kilometres ago, across the border it was. Licence please,' says the officer with a tone of arrogance. The cop walks away and back to his highway patrol car and gets on the radio. He does the usual licence and criminal check and then comes back to Michael.

'Your record and licence are clean,' says the officer with a grunted dismay, 'I am issuing you with a speeding infringement. Cost of $375 payable within twenty-eight days, and a loss of three demerit points. Have a nice day and slow down,' says the cop.

Michael kept his mouth shut the entire time, just listening while his blood pressure was slowly rising, 'Oh, how I'd love to take that gun and bash you senseless, you dumb fuck,' he thinks, all the while maintaining a poker face. The cop goes back to his car and just sits there, as if waiting for Michael to do something else – something wrong.

He is already quite angry with his victim getting away last night, this is something that will only deepen his mood. He is dark and sultry and looking for revenge, things aren't going right and someone will pay, and soon. Until then it is back on the road with a closer watch on his speed.

Back at Sutton Forest, he needs to refuel and eat. He's grateful for the company fuel card, as the total cost of $192 to fill up was more than he'd be happy to pay. Not wanting to waste any time, he goes to the convenience store and grabs some pre-made sandwiches, a large bottle of coke and the daily newspaper. As he is slowly walking back to the truck, he is approached by a man in his midtwenties with a backpack on who asks if he is headed north. The guy is heading for Bowral on his travels around the country.

'Yeah, mate as a matter of I am, where are you going?' Michael asks.

'A small country town called Bowral,' he replies.

'I pass by there so if you are ready now I'm happy to give you a ride,' says Michael.

'I have a friend if that's alright,' he says as the friend walks towards them.

'Oh ok, I can fit you both in,' Michael says.

There is a comfortable silence in the truck as Michael manoeuvres out of the complex driveway and back onto the highway. With Van Halen pumping, Michael is in a considerably good mood considering the way his day started. Ominous clouds are starting to form in the morning sky and he hopes that there is no thunderstorm brewing behind it.

'So, you guys are trekking around Australia, hey? Where were you coming from?' asks Michael.

'Well, we started in Melbourne last week,' says the guy who had approached Michael. He has a thick Irish accent and Michael has to listen closely so that he can understand exactly what is being said. 'Oh, and pardon me for being rude, I'm Paddy and this is my sister Felicity. We are from Dublin, Ireland, and visiting family as well as sightseeing,' says Paddy.

'Glad to meet you both, I'm Michael. Born and bred in Sydney. I'm coming back from Adelaide for work,' Michael says.

'We're doing a round trip and Adelaide is our last stop before we go back to Melbourne to fly home. We have never met our family in Australia. Most of them are on our Da's side though we have seen plenty of photos of them,' says Paddy. 'My father is a boat builder as was his father and father before. But I'll be buggered if I'm gonna build any bloody ship. My great grand da was born in Belfast, and worked on the Titanic, and was a young man at the time. We have lots of photos back home,' Paddy continues.

Michael is soon regretting picking these two leprechauns up. 'Man this guy could talk underwater with a mouth full of marbles and you'd still be able to understand every word clearly,' he thinks to himself.

'. . . and while we were in Melbourne, a place called Dandenong, sounds more like a flower to me, we met a cousin who came to visit us in Ireland,' Paddy finishes.

'Oh, would you look at that over to your left guys, there's got to be at least thirty kangaroos in that field. Want to stop and take some photos?' says Michael.

'Oh, now that would be mighty kind of you, Michael. The family back home will just love this,' says Paddy.

So, Michael pulls up about fifty metres back from where the kangaroos are gathered, most of them are just lying on the ground enjoying the sun, while a few are slowly moving about looking for food. There isn't much around with the grass almost bare here. Some areas are drought affected and this is one of those places. Paddy and Felicity unpack their cameras and attach a zoom lens, so that they can get in closer and snap up some amazing wildlife photos for the family back in Dublin.

CRACK. That sound echoes across the field and Paddy turns to find out what made that awful bone crunching bang. No sooner does he halfway turn around – his jaw explodes. Felicity is already on the ground, unconscious, and Paddy is doing everything within his power not to pass out. Michael takes another swing and Paddy raises his left arm to protect himself from the steel pipe that Michael has grabbed from the tray of the truck and breaks his arm in two places. Paddy screams out in agony and Michael swings again, this time hitting him in the temple and knocking him out.

Michael gets himself into a more comfortable position and then pounds into Paddy, breaking several ribs, smashing his skull in and completely tearing his jaw off with one almighty final blow. He now turns his focus onto Felicity – she stirs just a little as she begins to wake. With Paddy out of the way, he can now take his time torturing her.

He taunts her by walking around her mumbling how it's all her fault. If she hadn't left him all alone this would never happen. Of course, she has no clue what he means or who he's talking about and is scared beyond belief. One minute they are enjoying the scenery and about to take some beautiful photos, and the next thing she knows she is fighting for her life. The back of her head is split open and blood is oozing down the nape of her neck and into her blouse.

Michael continues this pattern for as long as ten minutes, banging the steel pipe against her arms and legs, making her flinch and squeal each time, in between the sobs and sniffling. 'Quit your fucking sniffling, bitch, that's driving me mad,' he yells at her. She can't help it – the sobs just won't stop and her nose has been bleeding for a little while now. Michael is finally fed up with her sniffling and with the force of a wrecking ball, he slams the steel pipe across the side of her face, breaking her cheek bones and eye socket.

She collapses in a heap like a sack of potatoes, and he just looks at her with her right eye almost hanging out. Unsatisfied with himself, he swings the pipe a few more times, grinning as each hit breaks more bones. He has been fortunate, because in his fury on the side of the road, there has been no passing traffic. Realising this he quickly drags both of the bodies to the side of his truck, where by chance if anyone drove past, all they would see is a truck driver checking his load and smoking a cigarette.

The challenge now is where to place the bodies. He scans the area very carefully with hawk-like eyes. There is an area that drops off but it is quite hard to see unless you are looking for it. The way the grass grows in some parts has created an illusion that the ground is actually flat, and the way that he noticed this, was that a kangaroo popped his head up – at first, it just looked like a rock until it moved. He does a thorough check for any traffic before he starts, it being so quiet here, he can hear oncoming traffic from a good distance away.

Getting the bodies into the little ditch area was no real effort, the blood was the only thing that he had to try and avoid. Though he already has an explanation for that if he is asked, he hit a kangaroo and it became wedged in the truck's bull bar, so he got blood all over him trying to dislodge it. He would have to pull over at the first car wash and gurney the front of the truck, so as to show that he had to clean the mess before it began to stink to the high heavens.

The wonderful thing about nature and gum trees is that branches are always falling, so the whole effort took no more than ten minutes, gathering as many fallen twigs and branches with which to moderately cover the bodies – maybe a few foxes might come along and help remove some of the evidence. He'd built up quite a lather of sweat getting the task done as quickly as possible. He has already spent too much time off the road; making it up without speeding will be a challenge, so it's non-stop back to work. But, what to do with their belongings. He'll just have to take them with him for now and keep them in the back of the truck, covered in a blanket taken from Paddy's bag.

He keeps a small water tank underneath the tray, along with an industrial hand cleaning cream, using this to lightly wash himself over and giving his hands a really good scrub. After this is done, he climbs up onto the back of the truck, takes a good look at the area where his adventures have taken place, and looks at it through the eyes of passing motorists. With nothing looking unusual or out of the ordinary, he jumps down and shakes off the killer in him, he composes himself and sets off for home.

He is almost home, and takes the Campbelltown off-ramp to the industrial area hoping to find an industrial bin to dump the belongings of his latest victims. It's just past sundown and all the factories are closed for business for the day. He is almost all the way through the industrial park when he spies a huge industrial bin left out ready to be emptied, more than likely before the start of business, the next day.

He gladfully disposes of the stuff that will only raise questions if someone was to move his truck before he starts his next shift after getting back. A sense of relief washes over him, and he feels that he has done enough killing for a little while. The last one really took it out of him, to the point where he actually questioned whether or not he went too far this time. He might just have to take a break for a while, besides the warmer days are becoming less frequent, and he certainly is not a fan of the cold.

He is back at the yard and it is empty, so he unlocks the gate and parks his truck in the usual place, right beside that big old tree. He feels so completely drained that he isn't even sure if he can make the forty-minute drive home. Despite his exhaustion, he pushes on and makes it home without nodding off at the wheel. All the lights are out at home, so he creeps in as quiet as a church mouse, goes into the bathroom and not the en-suite to brush his teeth, then goes to bed and cuddles up to Louise.

The next day he sleeps in. Louise tries twice to wake him, and he says that he is not feeling well and is taking the day off to recover. What from she isn't exactly sure of; he has done long-distance driving before and never had the next day off after getting back. She rings Jordan and explains the situation. Jordan says that he hadn't expected Michael back until late that day so it was fine. He would prefer Michael to get some rest and be back in shape soon.

Michael wakes a little after midday and the first thing he does is to make a coffee. He was about to go out on the back steps to light a cigarette, an old habit, but strangely he no longer has a desire to smoke. With a coffee in his right hand, he wanders into the lounge room and puts the radio on, mainly for background noise as the house is so empty, and puts his feet up, reflecting on the many recent events.

A short time later, the hourly news report comes on and the DNA evidence confirms the identification of the body found just north of Batemans Bay. 'Further evidence has been discovered and though the police will not release any further information, they say that they are close to an arrest.' Michael has a curious grin because the police have already spoken with him, and therefore they must be looking at someone else. Only time will tell.

13

CHANGES

- - - - - - - -

After Michael returned from the Adelaide trip, he took the rest of the week off work, he just needed time to unwind and touch base with his inner self, to reflect on the last six months of his life. He is forty-nine years old and has had a good life. He grew up in a loving family with three siblings – a younger brother and two younger sisters, and parents who provided a comfortable lifestyle. He never wanted for anything, as his parents provided everything – a good education in a private school, clothing to suit the fashion each year or at the very least to suit their tastes. So there seems to be no logical reason for the seven murders he has committed.

They went on a family holiday at least once a year and sometimes they went overseas to places like Disneyland or Bali. At Christmastime, Santa always left the presents that they asked him for, in their letters to him – that is, until they got old enough to know that Santa was not so real after all – then they got wise and asked their parents for slightly more expensive or elaborate gifts. Birthdays were no different, with lavish parties, inviting all of their friends, and only one gift from each family member. There were plenty of gifts from their friends to keep them happy, along with some fabulous memories.

Michael's father was a civil engineer by trade and owned a building company in Sydney called Hubert Engineering. He initially started his career in Brisbane, Queensland, as a civil engineer, until he was given the opportunity to work for a major building company in Sydney. It was only a matter of less than six years, before his father, Kenneth Hubert, found himself in a financial position to start a business for himself. Some of the guys he had worked with over the years followed him and helped to build the business, which was recently rated as the fourth-largest building company in Sydney and tenth in Australia.

Michael's mother was a legal secretary and also earned quite a good income. Sadly, due to always having such a busy work schedule, she didn't get to spend a lot of time with her children. Though Kellie doted on her children, she felt that her career was very important so as to provide a financially stable environment and future for her children. Both Kenneth and Kellie, interestingly having the same initials, decided to hire a live-in housekeeper who would also work as a nanny for the family. They chose to do this after the last child was born, and Kellie was back at work full-time, which made Michael nine years old at the time.

Michael began to feel a separation from his parents, though his love for them never waned, he just seemed to notice the distance caused by their work. This never affected his ability to do well in school. He was chosen to be the valedictorian for his end-of-school graduation, and also during his years in high school, he played in the school's star rugby league team, which won a few seasons. Academically he did well in school, which begs the question: Why is he a truck driver and not in a more professional field? Michael is an intelligent man who has the ability to achieve in any field of work, but after seeing what it did for his parents, he swore that if he ever had a family, he would never let work take time away from his family. He cannot honestly remember a time when his father played catch or taught him to shave or drive a car. Money was never an issue; you want to learn to drive – here's the money. You want your first car – there's the money.

What was lacking was the warmth and love that he so desperately craved. The only time he ever had any real interaction with his father was when they went on holidays. One thing he did learn while on holidays was how to fish, how to tie the various knots and what sinkers and hooks were needed for different fish types. Apart from that, anything Michael learned in life, he taught himself through trial and error.

The housekeeper was only young herself and was still fairly new to her chosen career. Fresh out of high school, Elizabeth 'Lizzie' Wilson started to do a course in child care at her local college, and as far as house cleaning goes, Lizzie's mother was a dust Nazi. She was so fastidious with keeping the house clean that on weekends, instead of being able to go out with her friends, she was made to help clean the house. 'Cleanliness is next to Godliness,' her mother always said. Though there were times when she absolutely loathed her mother and wished her dead, she was so used to her mother's ways that she knew better than to fight her, and so it became a habit with cleaning.

Shortly before Lizzie's twentieth birthday, she saw the advertisement in the local paper looking for a live-in nanny and housekeeper. Lizzie had been with an agency that specialised in this field and had a great reputation. So, when she applied for the position, given the credentials of the agency, she was hired. Though the parents were initially concerned about her age and reluctant to hire her, she dressed sensibly, not like a lot of young girls today, she also presented as a very mature and switched on person. So, it was the reputation of the agency that convinced them to give her a fair chance. As far as they knew, up until the day she left, Lizzie conducted herself professionally, and the children liked her. So, when she left, they wrote her an outstanding reference. How little they knew, simply because Michael was too scared to talk.

The day Lizzie started at the Hubert residence, Michael instantly took a disliking towards her, he didn't exactly know why, but he could tell that she wasn't as nice as she made out to be. Maybe the sly grin or a look in her eyes, but there was a hidden evil that lurked on the surface just waiting to get out. For the first few months, Lizzie was an angel, the house was kept spotless clean, the children were fed regularly and the cooking was quite good. Another skill taught to her by the woman she called mum. The two youngest children were always read bedtime stories and tucked in, while the other two were old enough to take themselves to bed. Well, that was her opinion.

Soon the evil would begin and its main focus was on Michael. Being the oldest, she wanted him out of her hair. He was a nuisance to her and she felt that he got in the way. That he shouldn't even be here. Why she concentrated on him alone he never knew, but the impact of her actions would have dire ramifications later on in his life. Lizzie was kind and sweet to his younger siblings, and because he was the oldest, he claimed that he could stay up for a half more than the others. So, she allowed him to stay up while she tended to the young ones, then came downstairs to begin her reign of terror. Once the children were put to bed, Lizzie would tie a small scarf over Michael's mouth and then tie his hands behind his back. This way nobody could hear him screaming and he couldn't undo the scarf. She would then drag him to the small closet under the stairs that lead to the upper level of the house, and throw him inside, leaving the light switched off, so it was all dark and scary. Occasionally just for fun, she would pinch him on the arm, just near the soft flesh close to the armpit, where if she did happen to mark him, it would be hard to find.

Each time she did this, she told him that if he told his parents, well, she would have to bash his head in, so, being scared beyond belief he kept his mouth shut. There was one night when Kellie asked Lizzie if she had seen anyone harassing Michael lately, as he seemed to be quieter than usual. She said that one of the boys from school had been picking on him, but she was working with him to counteract it. The next night as she threw him into the closet, she hit him over the back of the head with a rolling pin and almost knocked him unconscious. 'I told you not to say anything to your parents, and now your mum is questioning me; perhaps, this will remind you to keep your snooty little mouth shut, you horrid little upstart,' she said, as she closed and locked the door behind her.

She was definitely not all there, because while Michael was tied up and locked away, she would sit and watch TV until late and then unlock the closet door to find Michael asleep. She would gently and carefully untie him then carry him upstairs and tuck him into bed. There were some mornings when Michael woke and thought that he had dreamt of being locked in a cupboard, until he saw the small bruising inside his arms and quietly cried.

This traumatic situation continued for about three years because as Michael got older, he also got stronger. Finally, Lizzie could not hold Michael down and he became defiant, he pushed her hard against the wall, almost denting it with her shoulders. He also stood taller than her and told her that it stops now. With her tail between her legs, she knew that her days were numbered and it was time for a change. Lizzie left the residence two weeks later, stating that she needed a change of scenery and was contemplating a career in hospitality.

The agency soon found a replacement for Lizzie and things quickly calmed down for Michael. The new housekeeper was an older lady with over twenty years' experience and welcomed Michael as well as his siblings, treating them as if they were her own. The horror that Michael endured was forgotten a few years later with the calm and loving environment at home. Almost immediately, his moods got better and he was making jokes and appeared to be a happier young man. His mum saw this change as a teenage thing, slowly growing into his own.

Now that he is close to his middle age, Michael finds himself pondering his past. Deep in thought, he has begun to get a better understanding of why he feels like he does, a deep-seated anger that had been hidden for far too long. He has seen a connection that he previously didn't recognise until now. His victims are quite young and usually in their early twenties, with light or sandy coloured hair, just like Lizzie. It is quite often the smug way the girls walk and talk that catches his eye and peaks his interest in them, and he knows that he has to put the rubbish out. To dispose of the trash that psychologically twisted his otherwise good sense of judgement and balance in life.

What has left him puzzled is what has triggered the urge to kill NOW – not only that, but why is murder the answer to his darkness. For all the years people came in and out of his life, whether young or old – there was opportunity aplenty – Why is he striking with vengeance now? Regardless of the reason, he knows it is time to make a few changes for now, take a break from the horrible things he has done, and lie low. Besides, he is no fan of the colder seasons, so the opportunity to be a better person has come at a good time. Nobody has to know what he did, and as far as he is concerned, he had been careful and tidy.

While he considers his current position, he needs to come up with a plan. A set of explanations for timelines and other information that may be required. He still suspects that the police will further interview him in regard to the first murder. If no other bodies are found – hopefully, never – he feels confident that he can convince the authorities of his innocence in the matter. If more bodies are discovered, he plans to just play it cool and be cooperative, so as to avoid suspicion. After all, he has not left any clues – at least he doesn't think he has.

14

THE CALM BEFORE THE STORM

Winter followed autumn and this year it was exceptionally cold. There were several mornings when Michael went to his car only to find it covered in a thin layer of ice, and then he had to painstakingly scrape the ice off the windshield with a kitchen spatula. He could never remember when it mattered, to buy a plastic scraper from the hardware store near his work and keep it in his glove box. So, with numb fingers he set about clearing the ice.

This particular morning, he was lucky to find the windows clear of ice from the morning damp; this allowed him the luxury of getting to work earlier, which was nice for a change. With the wet weather of late, it felt like people had forgotten how to drive, by driving slower and a little more cautiously. So, when he spent more time than he wanted by scraping ice off his car, he arrived late on a number of occasions. This frustrated him somewhat but it didn't get the better of him. He now has control over his urges, in fact, he hasn't really had any urges since he took the time to sit and reflect on his life.

Thankfully, with winter now nearly over, Michael can start to feel human again. It was too long and too cold, and he is looking forward to getting back to wearing shorts and singlets. With only a week or so before spring, he has had the opportunity, and used it successfully, to pick up people hiking to their destinations without any inkling or desire for murder. Three weeks ago, there was a little activity by the police as they think that they have a link between two murders, though the areas in which the bodies were found seems irrelevant. Both bodies were badly beaten around the skull with a blunt object, most likely a pipe of some sort. The weapon used in both the incidences was never recovered, and so, they could only speculate what type of material was used.

The body that was found earlier in the Bulahdelah area was found by the property owner, as the news report said earlier in the year. Her identity picture was released to the public two months after she was discovered, because she was not listed on the missing persons list. No family came forth in the early stages, and as yet, nobody has been forthcoming in identifying who she is – just another Jane Doe in the long list of missing people.

Both cases went cold when the police were unable to make an arrest; forensic evidence was of little help. Thankfully, no DNA tests were done from the first victim – there had been several types of cigarette butts around the deceased, as Michael had left a butt at the scene. And due to the variety of them, the police only collected a few of each brand to be used in evidence. The delivery docket was all that they had from the Batemans Bay case and after interviewing all of the drivers; they all had convincing reasons for the possibility of it being found somewhere near the body. The police didn't push too hard on this matter as the distance between the body and the document was about three metres apart, meaning that it was likely that the document had flown out of the passenger side door, as stated.

For the six months of autumn and winter, Michael honestly didn't have any desire to kill. And as he is driving out west to Oberon to pick up a load of timber, he starts thinking about why. He recalls the story of Lizzie, but it just doesn't make sense to him, why the desire only in the warmer climate. It's a bitter cold day today, as he drives through the Blue Mountains area and he decides to switch the truck's heater on to make the journey more comfortable. No hitchhikers today either. Though winter is almost over, it's far too cold to be wandering around in this godforsaken weather. The winds are so strong that at one point, and on a tricky bend, he could feel the wind pushing against the truck, rocking it to and fro. He thought he saw snow as well, though it was only icy rain. This made the roads a little slushy to drive on, so caution was needed.

BANG – it hit him. When Lizzie used to lock him in the room under the stairs, it was early summer. And a hot summer in a dark, stuffy room meant it was overly claustrophobic. Some nights were stifling in there, and he would come out of the room drenched in sweat, his shirt sticking to his back from where he would sit leaning against the wall, alone in the darkness, quietly crying to himself. How he hated her, how he wanted to make her pay. Well if she couldn't pay, someone else would. Suddenly, Michael was just too hot to deal with the drive and put the driver's side window down. The ice-cold wind on his face was like an orgasm, the explosion of calm that ascended upon him was more relaxing than he expected. Feeling euphoric, he confidently continued his drive for a good few hours before he reached his delivery point.

During this drive, he started thinking about the upcoming summer, if he is to commit the atrocities of last summer, he might just up the ante, maybe add a little twist here and there. He may even go outside the usual hitchhiker and find victims randomly. The hardest part of not being caught is the timing. With his job and family, he'll just have to play it by the ear and think of new methods, until he tires of the whole thing. 'I might even join a dating service on the internet, do it from Jords's office,' he says to himself, as he slowly climbs a steep hill. The truck is crawling at a snail's pace, and suddenly a myriad of thoughts fill his head. 'I might even offer to help Jords in the office two days a week, learn some of that paperwork that he bitches about all the time.'

It wasn't until nearly 6:00 p.m. that night that Michael returned to work, with very heavy peak-hour traffic – it only takes one car to break down and the traffic banks back for miles. He was grateful that Jordan was still in his office, as this gave him an opportunity to plant the seed needed to be able to work in the office. 'Hey, Jords, you're here late. I take it you have lots of paperwork still to catch up on, huh?' Michael says.

'Yeah, and lately, it's never ending. I'm getting tired of leaving so late at night,' Jordan replies.

'You know I was only thinking about that today, I've noticed over the last few weeks that you're getting out late,' Michael says. 'I've been thinking about having a change in my routine lately, I don't want to leave here, but I feel the need to mix things up a little bit,' he explains.

'What do you mean by change? What's wrong with what you are already doing?' asks Jordan.

'Nothing is wrong, in fact, I want to learn new things. I was thinking about this and it might just help you out as well,' says Michael.

'Seriously? And how do you think you could help me,' Jordan asks curiously.

'Well, if I can suggest something for you to think about – don't answer right away – but what if I could work in the office with you, say two days a week, doing invoicing or computer work. Help take the load off your back while I learn something new,' says Michael.

'That is actually a good idea. You think of that all on your own, huh?' he says jokingly. 'I will think about it and talk to HR, maybe we can organise something. I'll let you know next week,' says Jordan.

Now he just has to wait and hope his plan has worked out. If so, then when spring and the warmer weather starts, he can resume his new-found hobby, murder of the summer hiker.

15

NEW CHALLENGE

'Mike, when you get back from your run this afternoon, I need to have a meeting with you,' Jordan says.

'Sure thing, Jords, anything I should be worried about?' Michael asks.

'Nah, mate, just need to talk about your proposal. Shouldn't take long, either,' says Jordan. Michael is a little excited at the prospect of the company supporting him in his quest for revenge. He really hadn't expected this to be so easily accepted, however, there are still a few little challenges before he can really take advantage of the computer system at work.

Just how many dating sites he will join is yet to be determined, and how to juggle his home life with this new twist will take careful and considerate thinking out. The new position will mean that he will have to stay back at work on the odd occasion, but since the family has drifted apart a little, he doesn't see this as a problem.

So, all day while he was doing his deliveries, he kept creating different scenarios in his mind. The idea of creating a broader spectrum for murder excited him. The planning needs to be precise, no room for error, and disposal has to be absolutely thorough. The day seemed to drag, seconds felt like minutes, minutes felt like hours and hours – well, that felt like weeks. And yet, five hours later, he was back in the yard. After parking his truck under his favourite tree, and tidying up the interior, cleaning up the scraps of his snacks from the day, plus a few empty bottles of coke – a harmless addiction – he wandered into Jordan's office as he usually does, to file the delivery dockets in an alphabetical company order.

Jordan was not in the office when he walked in, so after he did his filing, he went into the kitchen lunchroom and made himself a cup of black coffee. The wait wasn't long and Michael was prepared for the meeting, but he hadn't expected the dragon lady from the human resources department to attend. Ruth Lane is a spinster and to Michael's knowledge she has never dated. She is a bitter woman in her early fifties, and quite honestly, he could not think of one single person who can stand being in a room with her for more than five minutes.

Strange as that may be, when it comes to business and organising people and tasks, she is such a lovely person, no doubt because she has total control of the given situation. When she is in a bad mood, though, it's safer to give her the widest berth and avoid her at all costs. In fact, he often expected to see a red light above her office door, the kind you might find in a recording studio, 'Keep Out-In Session,' so that staff knew when to simply come back later. Poor Donna from reception went in one day to confirm an appointment with a prospective employee and got her head literally bitten off. She was so distraught that she went to make a cup of tea to calm her nerves, and ended up spilling half of it by the time she got back to her desk.

So, it will be interesting to see how she interacts this afternoon. Jordan politely introduces her, 'You know Ruth from HR?' he asks.

'Yes, of course, how are you, Ruth?' Michael says.

She gives him a sly and distrustful eye and sits down not replying at all to his politeness. Suddenly, you could cut the air with a knife – Jordan clears his throat and asks Michael to take a seat.

'So, you want to learn the computer system, a man at your age,' she retorts.

Michael isn't holding back today and with the most polite and charming smile he replies by saying that a woman of her age can't talk. Suddenly, that breaks the ice and she is gentle and warm for the rest of the meeting. Michael assumed that she likes strong dominant men, or people in general, and feeds off the weakness of others.

'Yes, I do, Ruth, I've seen Jordan get caught up a lot lately and I have had a little spare time in the afternoon. I would normally help around the factory, but I have this desire to learn new tricks. I might be an old dog, but I'm not going to let that stop me,' explains Michael.

'When Jordan first came to me with this, I laughed. I thought he was joking until I realised that he had no smile on his face. So, I have looked at this carefully, and I can offer you two days a week, about two hours each of those days. This will not affect the hours you are already doing, and your pay stays the same for now. If you get the hang of things quick enough and can prove your worth, there might be more in it for you,' says Ruth.

Michael wasn't expecting any more than that to start with and was happy about the idea that there could be more in it later for him. The only problem he has now is alone time on the computer to join and research dating sites. But first things first, he will go along with the flow of learning the computer and keep to the work schedules. What the hell, six months of the year are warm enough for his pleasures, so he is in no hurry.

Three weeks have passed since his meeting with Ruth and Jordan, and already he is working completely unsupervised. Jordan couldn't be happier either, they both know Jordan piles the shit jobs onto Michael to fix, and truth be told, Michael loves it. Something that he wasn't entirely sure of whether he would at first. Louise doesn't seem to mind him coming home a half hour or so late, and Michael is happy to stay back a little, overtime is allowed, and this allows her that little extra drinking time away from prying eyes. She still drinks heavily and hides it well. Her new method of getting rid of the bottles is to go for a walk to a large park only two blocks away, where there are a few large bins. All she has to do is bag them, go for a walk and dispose of them thoughtfully. She walks the two blocks every day and everyone is none the wiser.

'Hey, Mike, I have to fly to Melbourne on Thursday to meet with a company interested in doing big business with us. So, tomorrow there will be no deliveries for you, as I want to train you up a little in the delivery procedures, organising routes and times for the guys. I have informed Ruth and said that you may need to do a few hours overtime, you ok with that?'

'Yeah, Jords, I can handle that. I look forward to the challenge,' says Michael. Here is his perfect opportunity to use the computer system. He'll wait until dragon lady goes home and then start looking at his options for the dating sites.

He found a list of them and was amazed at some of the names that he discovered; Cuddly Couples, FindMeNow, and Harmony4U topped the list of five, he then decided to try FindMeNow. He searched the internet for a photo to suit his profile, something that was close to his features without actually looking like him. He wanted the illusion of the photo being similar, so that when he met someone, he didn't look completely different from the profile photo. He set his age at just over forty, and in a part of his descriptions, he stated that he was interested in meeting with girls between nineteen and twenty-six for fun and company. He also stated that he was recently divorced and was not looking for a commitment, just someone to have a good time with. He now needs a username as well as a profile name, needing to keep his true identity as far from being known as possible, so after a long pause and coffee break, he came up with his new name, Timothy Gibson aka Timmo or just Tim, and the username as @Timmo319.

Now to lay in wait.

Almost immediately, he starts getting notifications of interest, yet he somehow thinks that it is an auto response from the site to peak his interest. So, while he is finishing his coffee he takes a look at some of the profiles and is surprised at how many young gorgeous girls are looking for guys. Back in his day, before the electronic age exploded, one way to meet a gal was at a bar or a nightclub. Nowadays, it's all electronic media. The decision to hold off responding to any of the notifications wasn't an easy one but he knew, timing is essential, and he simply felt that now isn't the time.

Time to log off the computer and head on home to see his family. Hopefully he isn't too late for dinner but if he is, he will have to deal with it then. He has been wanting to talk to Louise for a while about his dark moods but just cannot bring himself to do so. The new twist on things with the extra work has him both excited and worried. Lately, he wants revenge more than anything, but is fighting with the inner nice guy, the one that knows murder is wrong. He even contemplated speaking with the priest of his local church. He was trying to remember the last time he sat in on a confession, it must have been when he was still a teenager. It's been far too many years since he has been to church, and he isn't planning on going any time soon. So, for now it's just a matter of time, hopefully, not too soon, before he cracks from the weight of his wrong doings and changes his MO, so that he will eventually get caught.

He arrived home to find his daughters in a full-blown fight. Louise was screaming at them to stop and was in hysterics, but neither girl could her over their constant back and forth yells at each other. He had to duck because of a shoe that was thrown across the room towards the front door, and suddenly he yelled out, 'THAT'S ENOUGH! BOTH OF YOU!' He says it so loud that the windows almost rattled and actually scared the girls. They stopped, frozen in their tracks. 'What the hell is going on here?' he yells.

'Danielle started it, she said that you are responsible for Wayne's sister's death,' says Michelle.

'Well, that's what he said,' claims Danielle.

This actually caused him to freeze in his tracks. How could anyone have seen what happened? They were quite remote and he was certain that nobody else was around. Still, the idea of having been seen freaked him out, badly. A master of this skill, he found immediate composure, and did not, in any way, show that this was any concern of his, or theirs, and so went straight in to father mode. 'Whoa, back it up a little bit, firstly, Stephanie went missing, and we all know that. The fact that she hasn't been found is a very sad one, it's possible she drowned while swimming alone, but we might never know. Secondly, if you think I had anything to do with her disappearance, well, that is very upsetting, to think that you could even think that I am capable of doing anything sinister actually hurts,' he says. 'And besides, what the hell are you doing talking to that boy? I've told you to keep away from him,' he says quite angrily.

The look on their faces was one of shame. In unison – something that they've done for years and still amazes Michael – they both say sorry. He almost cracks a smile because of the way they said it, it sounded like a stereophonic speaker, with a certain harmonious ring to it. He insists that they apologise to each other and their mother – yet again they speak at the same time – and then he gives them both a big hug. Something about a big hug from daddy always made them feel better.

'Hey, D, let's go and play Sims on the x-box,' says Michelle. And with that, peace was restored. Michael and Louise retreated to the kitchen for a stiff drink before he sat down to eat. They sat quietly for a little while without saying a word, then Michael went on to explain a little bit about his new role at work. Of course, it was nothing exciting but he was happy to have something different to do at work, and she was happy enough to listen in her slightly inebriated state.

The following day, he spent most of the day as Jordan's shadow, learning how to organise delivery routes and how to compile the information on the computer. He also had a chance to speak with a supplier to order stock. This office thing was pretty cool and a refreshing change from the madness out on the road. It was one of those days where the clock ticked two minutes for every one minute, and before he was even aware, it was nearing time out. Clock punching time and heading out of the office.

16

BOWLED OVER

- - - - - - - -

The following few weeks after Michael took on the added role at work – now, officially titled Administration Assistant – everything seemed to be going well. He had a good mix of driving and office duties, and his family life was a happy one. Though, it took a little bit of work to smooth things out with Danielle. She somehow felt that the rumour going around school – petty troublemakers stirring the pot – that her father had somehow been involved in Stephanie's disappearance, had a ring of truth to it. She has kept this little secret to herself for quite a while, one that may surface sooner than she expects, now that she saw her father bludgeon the next-door neighbour's small dog to death. The Jack Russell would climb under a small gap in the fence and make a mess of the garden in his backyard. A garden her father took pride in, as he had spent weeks digging and planting to get it just right. On one occasion, a few plants had been uprooted, and he was furious – he stormed over to the next-door neighbours and demanded an apology, needless to say that with his attitude he never received it. So, he swore revenge.

Michael lives in a two-story home where Danielle's bedroom looks directly on to the backyard. This particular afternoon on a hot summer's day, Michael had come home from work, got a cold beer from the fridge and proceeded to go out to the backyard and water the plants. To his horror, the dog was nose deep in dirt with a grevillea ripped out of the ground. He quietly placed his beer on the outdoor setting and passively walked over to the dog, picked it up by the scruff of the neck with his left hand, pulled his right hand back and with all his might, and punched the poor pooch with one hit, so hard, it gave one tiny yelp and went limp. He dropped the dog, got down on his knees and kept punching the dog until every bone was broken. Afterwards, drenched in sweat, he went to the garden shed to get a shovel, and dug a hole about three feet deep and buried the next-door neighbour's dog, and then went about replanting the grevillea and tidying up the loose dirt. Occasionally sipping his cold beer as if nothing more than a little gardening was all he did.

Meanwhile, upstairs, Danielle had been working on a school project, writing an essay about an Egyptian god or goddess, complete with drawings of the era, when she heard the dog yelp. So, she went to the bedroom window curious to see if it had hurt its foot, when she saw her father had grabbed the dog with a crazed look on his face – she immediately closed the curtain with just a slither of an opening. She watched in horror, the whole thing being unfolded right before her eyes – it seemed like a nightmare, only in the daytime instead of the dark of night.

So, it was due to witnessing her father's atrocity on the poor adorable dog, somebody's pet, that she had her suspicions and found it hard to believe otherwise. It took a little convincing on Michael's part, by explaining the story, one he made – that was very likely and plausible – about his involvement in the search party – the items they found and brought back. 'Now, why would I bring items back to the group of people gathered to find her, if I had anything to do with it? Surely it would make sense that if I found anything at all, I would want to hide it so that it would make it harder to find out where she had been,' he said convincingly. Among other similar conversations with Danielle, she eventually forgot about the whole thing. After all he wasn't a violent man, he went out of his way to provide for the girls. He even tried playing computer games with them where he would lose, and badly, but make jokes about it until they were on the floor in fits of laughter.

So, yeah, it was all going well.

Tonight is Friday night drinks with the boys at work and he declined to go so that he could spend the time with his family. With the extra work, he doesn't get to spend as much time with them as he'd like, so tonight it's off to Bowlarama Ten Pin Bowling with as many snacks as they want. There is a little excitement in the air because tonight it's disco bowling with fancy laser lights and mirror balls. They also have a modern-day jukebox with the latest tracks, including 'Take My Hand' by the Bishop Boys. Apparently, they're all the rage and very popular with the teenage girls, with posters included in their CDs. He honestly doesn't get today's music – give him seventies rock any day.

The night is going well and after the first game – Michelle beat them all – Michael decided to go outside for a cigarette, though he has tried to give them up, he stills has the occasional puff. He could hear a whimpering voice coming from a distance to his left in the car park and thought he would investigate what it was. It so happened to be a young woman, possibly twenty–two, and sobbing. She has a flat tyre and has the tools lightly scattered around her.

'Hey, miss, what's wrong?' he enquires.

'I have a flat tyre but don't know how to change it, do you think you could help me, please?' she asks, between sobs.

'Yes, of course, I can. Now, let's see what we have here,' Michael says. In no time at all, Michael has the car jacked up and the spare tyre on, with the nuts tightened firmly enough to release the jack's support. He lowers the car and tightens the nuts firmly – and as quick as a flash, he swings around and hits the girl across the left temple with the tyre iron, causing her to fall to the ground unconscious. Without losing his momentum, he continues beating her around the skull until he sees brain matter through the blood.

Thank goodness, the car par was empty, and that this unsuspecting victim was parked in a relatively dark area, ironically not far from a dumpster. He was able to get his first taste of blood for the summer season, in a very quick and violent matter. He quickly goes to the dumpster, lucky for him it was the kind with lid supports, so that he was able to open the lid and then go and get the girl, dump her body inside and then close the lid again. Before he dumped her body, he had the mind to find her keys, in doing so, he was able to tidy the scene. Put the flat tyre into the boot of her car, pack away the tools and then collect anything that looked like it may raise suspicion, and dump that in the bin as well.

When he got inside the bowling alley, Louise asked what took him so long. He explained that there was a young lady with a flat tyre who had cut her hands trying to change it, and so, he gave her a helping hand. She could see what appeared to be grease or dark dirt, and small amounts of blood on his hands, so naturally, she believed him. He went to wash up and when he returned, the family continued playing bowling and having fun. And nobody had a clue what had just transpired in the very short space of time he was gone. When asked about the blood, he said the young girl had cut her hand badly, and he had tried to clean it up and wrap a bandage around the wound. Again, this was accepted and never discussed again.

At the end of the night, the staff went through the normal procedure of closing the bowling alley, except this night, the manager decided to empty the bins in the morning as it had started raining quite heavily and there was no shelter outside. This worked to Michael's advantage because the recycling truck arrived before sun up to collect and empty the dumpster, in among the trash, the dead girl was taken away.

At this particular recycling plant, trucks will reverse up to a bay and empty their waste which falls onto a large conveyor belt. This in turn carries the waste to a very large mulching area, with a massive wheel consisting of hundreds of teeth to really squash and mulch everything into a manageable pulp. With only one supervisor on site to oversee what goes on the conveyor, he somehow missed seeing the dead girl, as she was covered in refuse and very hard to see. This is one body that will never be found.

Three days pass and the Toyota Corolla is still in the exact spot it was the night the girl disappeared. The bowling alley manager called the police to report a possible stolen car that had been dumped in the car park, and a few hours later a squad car arrived to take details. The manager is quite frustrated because he had already given the details over the phone, and here he was, giving them again, to a dumb rookie cop as well. The senior officer stood back showing no interest in being there at all. He was standing in a leaning position against the side of the police car, while the new recruit carried on with her work. His duty today was to train and supervise the lackey who had a blunt attitude, and the bowling alley manager thought she was a good candidate for the job but kept his thoughts to himself.

'So, the car has been here for three days, is that right?' she asks.

'Well, I'd say so, I first noticed it on Friday night, but it wasn't until Saturday afternoon that I thought it odd that it was still there. As I didn't work on Sunday, I expected it to be gone. But as you can see, it's still here,' says the manager.

With a frustrated look on her face, the rookie cop jots down in shorthand the statement from the manager, then very bluntly says, 'Thanks, we will look into this, and if need be, we will organise a tow truck to collect the vehicle. Meanwhile nobody is to touch the car.'

With that done, they parted ways and got back to their own respective jobs.

Back at the police station, the information gathered by the rookie cop was handed to the investigations unit within the department and taken care of. The rookie had other duties to learn and was told that she had filing to do. Meanwhile, the investigations unit got started with the information handed to them. Firstly, by researching the licence plate number of the car to identify its owner. Khalie Davies, aged twenty-three years old, of Bankstown, was the owner of the car. A phone call was made to the residents of her address to enquire about whether or not the car was in fact stolen, and it was discovered that on Saturday morning, a phone call was made to Bankstown police station to report her missing. Suddenly alarms bells rang for the officer investigating the case, and they realised that they had a missing person's case now as well. So, it meant going back to the Bowling Alley to make more enquiries.

The investigation continued for a number of months before going cold. The staff at the bowling alley hadn't seen her, and with no cameras outside of the building, there was simply no evidence of her movements. It was unclear if she was kidnapped, if had she been there at all, or whether she met someone in the parking lot and went elsewhere in another car. The case was published in the local newspaper with only a few leads that went nowhere. All of her family and friends were also interviewed, with no results, though her family never gave up hope that she would be found. Sadly, for them, they will never find resolve, she will just be another missing person in a never-ending list that will never be found.

Michael saw the article in the local paper and felt satisfied with himself, knowing that if he was ever caught in his dark and evil ways, this is one that they could never pin on him.

Life was good.

The rest of the week Michael spent the afternoons at work doing his usual filing and organising delivery schedules for the next day, then when the office was clear, he would concentrate on responding to prospective internet friends on the dating site. He has been thinking about how he could possibly lure the young ladies into his lair. He figures that it will not be a frequent occurrence, so a cheap motel that is happy to accept cash, and not big on I.D., will suit him fine. A little research for next week. Right now, he is tired and just wants to put his feet up at home with a cold beer and watch the new fishing show Extreme Fishing with Dan Robson while the rest of the family go and visit Louise's brother, Simon. He can't stand the pompous upstart, the 'computer geek know-all technician.' They had a huge argument two years ago at a family picnic – Simon had been putting Michael down, by saying that his job was of a lowly roll, unlike his important role with Tempest Computers.

Tempest Computers has the contract to supply all the government schools with computers for all students. A technical system where all schools are interlinked with each other. This gives the government control of all curriculum and grading across the board, so that no school is disadvantaged in its existence. Simon is one of a few who have the job of monitoring and reporting this system to the local constituent, who in turn collates the entire collection of schools under his governing area, and forwards that to the Department of Education and Student Careers or DESC (pronounced desk).

Michael was understandably pissed off at Simon's attitude, though he understood the importance of this company's role in society, whereas Simon failed to take into consideration that if people like Michael did not deliver the necessary materials, then the schools would not even exist. Everyone plays an important part in the functionality of life, and in Michael's opinion, nobody was more important than anybody else.

So, he stayed home to a little solitude, where he could just be himself, whoever that was, and relax.

17

A DARK ROOM

He knows that the more evidence he leaves at a crime scene, the more likely it is for him to be caught. So, he has had to make a few changes in order to fulfil his hunger for murder. The fact that he has made a few changes since his first attack has without doubt kept the authorities guessing as to whether any of the few victims are linked somehow. A few remote similarities with each victim, specifically the manner in which they are brutally beaten around the head, and their age. Apart from that, there seems to be nothing linking them. They have nothing in common – one was an unemployed girl travelling, the other was on her way to stay with a friend. For now, as far as he knows, there has been no link to any murder and he hopes to keep it that way.

He found a motel in Lidcome, which is about ten minutes' drive from where he works, and it is ideal. It's dimly lit and situated next door to a brothel – he suspects that it is owned by the brothel, and they ask no questions. Their main clientele is the travelling truckie who needs a shower and a bed between trips, and the occasional John and Jane Doe paying for a room to get their thing on. He wonders how many marital affairs have started and finished there, but truthfully doesn't care. There are always rooms available at short notice, this he knows because he phoned them to make enquiries, stating that he was headed for Sydney from Brisbane at the end of next week, and needed somewhere to crash for a night, before he had to continue on to Melbourne.

Now he has to start telling lies to Louise about the overnight road trips, to cover why he will not be home, if he finds a likely candidate for murder. Well, no hurry yet, as he has not one person interested in meeting up with him after work. Ironic that he was thinking of road trips, when Jordan has one scheduled for him in a couple of days. He is always given a couple of days' notice so that he can let his family know, after all he does have a life and there may be times when he already has plans, and if this were the case, there is always someone else at work quite capable of doing the trip. This trip however is not an overnighter, a decent-sized joinery factory in Wauchope, just west of the fabulous Port Macquarie, has the contract to fit out a series of apartment blocks being built in Port Macquarie.

As usual, his truck is loaded up the night before to save wasting valuable time. Even with the new freeway bypassing many small coastal towns, the return trip, including unloading the truck, and depending on Sydney traffic, both on the way out and coming back in, could take up to nine hours. With a 7:00 a.m. departure, he should arrive in time for lunch. Even taking into consideration, having up to an hour for lunch, he should be back in the yard by the time Jordan is ready to close up and go home. This was the plan. Michael has driven this route so many times over the years, it's almost second nature. So, it took him by surprise when he had to take a detour through Raymond Terrace along the way, he hadn't gone through this little town in years. Apparently, there was a truck accident that closed the highway off in both directions, and the traffic was unusually heavy.

With the traffic moving at a crawling speed, he knew there was nothing that he could do, so as usual, whenever there is a delay, he phones the office to let them know that he will definitely be late getting back but will keep them posted as to his whereabouts. He never really gave it any thought, until now, that by keeping an open line of communication, he covers his tracks. If ever he is questioned about his events, he has

back up and support. The drive through Raymond Terrace is a short one at the best of times, driving past a Ford Dealership and a very old pub. In the distance, he can see someone walking along the road with their thumb cocked in a hitchhiker's gesture, which everyone has been ignoring. You just can't trust people today. Someone could be crazy and carrying a knife, or god forbid, a gun. Carjacking is slowly becoming a new mode of transport in this falling-apart world. Except for Michael, it works the other way around in this case. Hitchhike at your own peril. All risks taken, no responsibility accepted.

So, when Hannah accepted a lift, she had no idea it was to be her last ever.

The usual conversation flowed and everything seemed to be going well. Michael gave a brief description of himself and what he did for a living. Hannah was a twenty-year-old who lived in Newcastle. She had decided that before she turned twenty-one, she would try some camping and hiking, much to her parents' dislike. Hannah has always been a bit of a tomboy and could generally take care of herself, yet her parents still didn't like the idea of her going. Her stubborn nature prevailed and she went anyway, promising to call them every morning, which she did shortly before heading off again before she met up with Dr. Doom himself.

Her aim is to reach Southwest Rocks by that afternoon if the hiking works in her favour. She isn't bothered by how many people pass her by, without a glance – she has her MP4 player locked and loaded to keep her happy. So, when a driver does stop, she is cheerfully grateful to them, and says so. Most people are surprised to see this mix of a person, a very good-looking girl with a strong jaw line, and yet speaks like a bogan. She just tells it how it is, and occasionally apologises for her colourful language.

She is a bit of a chatterbox, which is ok in small doses, so by the time they reach the end of the detour and are back on the road, Michael pumps the stereo system to try and drown her out. She quickly gets the hint and put her earphones in to listen to her own music. That rock shit he is playing reminds her of her alcoholic father. Whenever he'd get drunk, if she were home, he would insist on her dancing with him, which then lead to sexual advances. Since she made it a point of hardly being home in the last six months, she was spared of his arrogant diatribe and persistence on her spending time with him.

How she grew to hate her father throughout her teenage years. He would get drunk and become loud, obnoxious and nasty, sometimes violent. There were times where she wagged school for a few days because she was going to school with a black eye or bruising, and that would definitely raise questions, questions she didn't want to answer. She basically told Michael all about this in the few short minutes before reaching the end of the detour, and somehow, she actually felt relieved. A calming sense of peace came over her, and after Michael cranked the stereo, she sat in a slouched position and began to nap.

Half an hour later – she is fighting for her life near a place called Old Bar, which is ironic due to the fact that an old bar is one of his weapons of choice. She was rudely woken by a punch to the lower jaw that brought stars to her eyes. Disoriented and sleepy, she had lost her bearings as to where she was and mistook it for another beating from her father. She yelled out for him to stop it and received a massive blow to the side of her head, instantly knocking her out. Michael has a short steel handled four-pound hammer hidden behind the driver's seat. He keeps it in case the load comes loose, and he needs to nudge things in place before re-tightening the load. While Hannah was asleep, he remembered that it was there and that it would be perfect for what he needed. It didn't take much to get started either.

He pulled up in a parking bay area alongside the road, suitable only for two trucks or a few cars. She hadn't stirred at all so he unbuckled his seat belt, and reached across with a slap that woke her. Of course, in his left hand he had the hammer and swung it with light force. The weight of the hammer did the job he required, and then proceeded to go about doing what nobody knew about. He pulled Hannah away from the door as she was leaning against it, this way she wouldn't fall out when he got out and went around to open her door. Being a good height from the ground, Michael was able to sling her over his right shoulder and carry her behind a tight group of large gum trees.

He gently placed her in a sitting position against the tree, then went back to the truck to grab the hammer. When he returned to where she was sitting, he found her awake but dazed. He isn't so much into taunting his victims all the time, he prefers to just smash and run. After hearing her story, he felt that she had been tortured enough in the past, but as she reminded him of his horrid babysitter and her plight as a teenager, he somehow felt more enraged than he normally would. Time wasn't exactly on his side, though this didn't stop him from bringing the hammer down hard on both of her ankles. He couldn't afford for her to get up and run. After securing his victim, he then went about hitting her around the face and head, breaking bones as he went. The more she sobbed or cried, the more pain he would inflict until he got bored with her. He finally brought the hammer down to the top of her head with one crushing blow that finished her off. Hannah drew in her last breath, crying out to her mother.

He went back to the truck to get her belongings and walked over to where she lay slumped against the tree, and with all of his strength, he threw her things as far as he could, scattering them in the thick scrub. Afterwards, he examined the area and decided to gather some branches to lay over her body. Concealment wasn't such a big issue, as the lay of the land sloped downwards and away from the road, and being behind the trees, it made it harder to find her.

He knows that, in time, she will be found, but he isn't concerned about it at all. It will add to the mystery for the police and make their job harder. What he failed to consider was that her parents would report her missing and give a detailed description of where she was headed. The police may then put a small search party out to locate her whereabouts and learn of the similarities between the other bodies.

The following morning, when Hannah failed to call her parents, they were only a little concerned, she could have slept in or was hung over, or just busy. So, they waited until late that afternoon. Still not having heard from their tomboyish and stubborn daughter, they began to worry. By sundown, they decided to call the police and file a missing person's report. It was then a waiting game to find out if she would call or be found.

Three days later she was found, far sooner than Michael anticipated, and the police collected all of her belongings after doing a thorough search of the area in which she was found. After several hours of investigating the surrounding area, they were unable to find any clues as to how she got there or who inflicted so much pain and damage on her. Hundreds of photographs were taken for future scrutiny, though nothing more came from this. Michael was careful not to leave any cigarette butts around or anything else that might lead them to conclude that he was involved.

Michael had finally returned to the yard at work by 7:40 p.m. that night and parked his truck under the tree as he always has. After driving out of the yard, he got out of his car, locked the gate and went home. The family were huddled together on the lounge watching some stupid reality show, so he quietly said hello, went upstairs to shower and then went to bed. Tomorrow had been a new day, with new adventures.

18

AN ACCOMPLICE

- - - - - - -

Jenny was her first internet date. A twenty-four-year-old who had been through a lot in life. The oldest of four children from a broken family, and rarely, if ever, would see her father. Bitter sibling rivalry and fighting caused her to drift away from the family to the point where she lived alone and had nothing to do with any of them. She has had a few relationships that never went anywhere, though she did get engaged once, but the guy was an abusive drunk who beat her one too many times. He strangely disappeared one day and had never been found.

Now she is looking for companionship once again, perhaps this time someone like a father figure. The younger guys just don't get what it is she wants, and they are unable to see who she is as a person. It's always all about them, and so, she is turning that around – if, after a few weeks, there is no chemistry, she will kick their sorry arse to the curb. And then there was Michael. They spoke for a few nights on the dating site and she felt quite comfortable with him, and therefore agreed to meet up with him in secrecy. He told her that he is married and not looking for a commitment or a relationship per se, though his profile states that he is divorced. This pleased her, as she could get some older company, with hopefully a little sex thrown in occasionally, without the commitment and stress of a relationship.

'Louise, honey, I have a trip to Melbourne on Friday and won't be back until Saturday afternoon,' he says.

'Oh, ok, Michael, then I might take the girls to go see my mum and stay the weekend,' she replies.

Michael loves the fact that she doesn't get upset that he is going to be away, and this is the first time that he is actually lying to her and staying in Sydney. He's not worried about it either, as for the last five months they have not slept together sexually, nor have they shown any real passion towards each other. He knows that she is still drinking and yet says nothing.

She has her alcohol and he has his victims, so he feels that they are kind of even in their flaws. In fact, they haven't been intimate since they got back from the Whitsundays – it really shook Louise to the core. She made the terrible mistake of putting herself in Stephanie's mother's shoes and sank into a mild state of depression. She couldn't imagine losing one of her children and was so distraught for the family. Because she never spoke of her feelings or concerns, she masked her woes with alcohol. She enjoyed the buzz that she got from drinking, and it quickly took hold of her.

So, Friday night rolls around and Michael leaves from work in the usual manner. If he left his car at work, it would only raise questions. He would normally leave it there when travelling interstate, and as this is what he told his wife, it would have been a given. However, with his new quest, he has to be careful not to be seen leaving work in a different direction. A slight detour only adds a few minutes to the trip to the Oasis motel, and on his way, he stops to grab some take away food for two. Though, he never bothered to ask Jenny. He opts for Thai food, only two blocks from the motel, so it all works well with the timing.

Jenny arrives at 6:45 p.m. and Michael already has dinner served, ready on the little two-seater table. He serves up dinner using the plates in the little kitchenette of the room. The TV is on with some boring topic of medical fraud on a current affairs program, though he isn't taking any notice. While they eat, sitting quietly, he notices Jenny staring at him with a cute grin. She finds him strikingly handsome and strong, judging by his build. She thinks she has found her man, but won't jump to any conclusions just yet. He still has to pass the test.

Later that night, Michael had intended to murder her, he had it all planned out in his head, but there was something about Jenny that he couldn't quite put a finger on. There was a certain mystery that intrigued him. Throughout the night they had been discussing their past, Jenny was quite open while Michael was more reserved. On top of her estranged family, Jenny's mother suffered from bipolar disorder and was often quite violent around the house. Sometimes, she would lock all four of her children in the small laundry, a small room with no window, cold and damp and that smelled of a mix of chemicals, bleach being the strongest odour. One really cold day, in the middle of winter, she locked them all in because two of them were fighting over which breakfast cereal they wanted. She lost it, locked them away and got drunk. She went on a two-day bender and totally forgot the children – when she finally let them out, they had all soiled their clothes and were found in tears.

Her mother apologised for days after that horrible experience, but Jenny never forgot. Three years later, Jenny poisoned her mother by putting rat poison in her food. Needless to say, her mother died a nasty death and nobody was able to prove where the poison came from or who administered it. This got Michael thinking about his situation – sometimes he wishes he had killed his babysitter, then he may not have committed murder on the poor innocent girls who fell victim to his evil ways.

They sat and talked for a few more hours, when out of character, Michael reaches across and kisses Jenny. Not on the forehead, and not on the cheek either, but smack bang on the lips. He felt turned on by her story and the urge overcame him. Jenny responded in kind, and suddenly like the tearing down of an old, abandoned building, they tore each other's clothes off and had the wildest sex Michael had ever experienced. They made love a few times during the early hours of Saturday morning before falling asleep.

Michael wakes, startled, that horrible feeling that you don't know where you are is a strong one. He looks across at the small alarm clock beside the bed and sees that it was 8:33 a.m. and looks around the room. The bed is empty and the room is dark. At some point, Jenny had quietly gathered her things and left. He lights a cigarette and gets up to make a strong black coffee, then sits down and thinks about what just happened. Did he actually have sex with a woman he had just met? According to the condom wrapper on the floor, he did. He waited for the wave of guilt but it never came. Feeling good about his actions, he handed the keys for the room to the guy behind the reception desk and left to go home. Upon his return to his humble abode, he relished the peace and quiet. His back patio had a swing chair at one end, resting parallel with, and facing the house, with a small TV attached to the wall. The sports channel had the car races on with a variety of events, from the V8s to rally car driving. So, he cracks a cold beer and settles in for a relaxing afternoon.

After a light lunch and a few more beers, he has a nap, which turns out to be a long sleep. He dreams of being at a small lake, fishing for trout, a thunderstorm brewing overhead. He turns to pack up his fishing gear and is shocked to see a faceless figure standing in front of him, holding a large claw hammer. As the hammer swings down, the dream changes, and it is he who is holding the hammer, no longer by the lake but on a sugar cane farm. He begins chasing a woman who is in her mid-fifties, only to lose her. He works his way out of the crop, into daylight, staring directly into Jenny's face. Her hands are covered in blood and there is sweat on her brow – she tells him, 'It's ok, we can do this together.'

He suddenly wakes, drenched in sweat, and immediately goes to have a shower to cool himself down, in the hope that his nerves would quickly calm down. As he is showering, the family comes home and is puzzled by why he is home so early, considering that he wasn't meant to be home until later that night. While he was showering, and, yes, he heard them come home, he had time to come up with a plausible lie. After he gets out of the shower and dries off, Louise questions why he is home a day early.

'Well, Hun, I got as far as Albury and was met by Johnny Crick from Victoria. The company I was delivering to was sending goods to my work. So, we swapped trucks, which we'll exchange later, and I drove back to work. I got home about a half hour ago, I guess, and after having a breather, I decided to shower. How's ya mum?'

Louise faintly replies, 'Yeah, she's good, sends her love . . .,' then wanders off to the kitchen to pour herself a glass of wine. She seems a little moody, but that was nothing unusual lately.

Back at work, and he is anxious to get to the computer to see if Jenny has contacted him. Since his dream he has been thinking of the possibility that maybe she could play a part in his game. She could persuade the girls to meet up at the Oasis motel and he could do his work there. The blood splatter will be an issue, so he needs to rethink his strategy – he will probably have to change his whole routine and method of operation. He has a few deliveries to take care of first, and then he is able to get into the office to complete the filing of last week's delivery dockets and sort out tomorrow's deliveries, before he could log into the dating site and contact Jenny.

During that day when he had been driving in the madness of Sydney's traffic, he had come up with a few ideas for murder. He will need the work computer to do a little research, and if he can find what it is he needs, he will need to have somewhere to have supplies delivered. He can't have the goods turn up at work, as it would raise questions, to which he has no answers, so tomorrow, it will be a trip to the post office to find out what is needed for a post box.

He thought Jordan would never leave, and this reduced just how much time he had to work with. A quick check and no correspondence from Jenny, so onto the next phase. The few items he needed were easier to find than he thought, and luck was on his side. A few blocks from a company that he delivers too in Artarmon, has just what he needs, and best of all, he can purchase the items over the counter and pay cash. All he needs to do is check their inventory levels on the computer the night before he has a drop out that way and pick it up. No questions, no paper trail, and no need for the post office either. Two days later, he receives a short message from Jenny saying that she has had time to think since they first met and wants to meet up again. She also apologised for sneaking out so early that morning, she was kind of freaked out a little, as she has never ever done anything of the sort in her life, and was more nervous than she expected to be.

He agrees to meet up with her the following week, but for lunch at a café nearby, instead of the Oasis motel. He won't tell her now, over the phone, but his interests lay in testing her trust levels. The game plan is to put in place a scenario of a murder he committed, but make it sound like a 'what if we could' situation. If she is comfortable with the idea, then he will leave her to contemplate on it and get back to her in a few days.

She does meet with him at a lunch café in a backstreet of bustling St. Leonards. It is decorated in a fifties rock 'n' roll theme, with pictures on the wall, of James Dean, Elvis Presley, Buddy Holly and Little Richard. There was an authentic juke box in the back corner playing Keep on Knockin' by Little Richard. Perhaps it was trying to say something. Over coffee and cheesecake, they quietly discuss the idea. She surprises him by telling him she has fantasied about killing people, but knows that she isn't strong enough to do it and get away with it.

Except, of course, the one partner she had and killed. Hitting him in the back of the head with a hammer killed him instantly, but getting rid of the body was the hard part. For, that took all the strength that she had. She knew of a dirt track out past Campbelltown where she dumped his body. It's a very remote place, and as yet, nothing has been said about it in the news. That was over two years ago. So, Jenny agrees that she should think about it. After they part company, Jenny goes back to work feeling accomplished by the meeting, not only has she met a ruggedly handsome man, but one who shares her thoughts on killing. Of course, she will leave it all up to him to organise, but she is happy to be a part of it.

When they met up again a week and a half later, he lays his ideas on the table. He doesn't mention the previous murders, as he still doesn't know how much he can trust her, but he also has a new method that would definitely need her assistance. Michael originally thought Jenny could somehow bring the girls to the motel room, but realised that it should be him that should lure young impressionable girls to the Oasis motel. And then, let the fun begin – he will do this through the website that he had met Jenny through. The difficulty will be getting a girl to trust him, but with a free meal and alcohol on offer, he imagines that won't be too hard.

Michael is careful with how he keeps in contact with Jenny, as he cannot have her contacting him ever, except, and only, through the dating site. He had considered creating a Facebook page, through which they could have had quicker access for communicating, but felt that it was just too risky. He also thought about a pre-paid phone – this was reasonable, he could always tell Louise that it was a work phone. That the company is putting a phone in every truck, and due to his extra responsibility, it is required that he keep it on his person at all times. The problem with this, of course, is if Louise decided to go through the phone and discover endless messages between the two, he would come undone. For now, he needs to concentrate on how to lure his next victim, his next poor unsuspecting victim. And it's not long before this happens.

Three days later, his boss tells him to take the day off because of how efficient his workload has become. He has caught up on everything on the computer, and the delivery schedules for the next day are all in order. Happy with this news, he gets in his car, starts the engine, and just sits there not knowing what to do. It's at a time like this when he wishes he could contact Jenny and do something together. He suddenly realises that he isn't thinking about his wife but of another woman. He throws the car into first gear, slowly drives out of the work car park, heads up towards the motorway, and decides on a drive up to Lithgow. He had suddenly remembered about that girl he had missed the opportunity for killing, and wanted to check the place out.

He calls Louise from his mobile phone – hands free naturally – he cannot afford to lose points on his licence, nor the hefty fine. Last he'd heard, the fines were around $600 for getting caught using your phone while driving.

'Hi, darlin'. I have a delivery to make this afternoon, last minute and urgent. I am going to Lithgow and will stay overnight in the pub. I think it's called The Highway Hotel if ya need me . . .yeah, love you too. Bye, love,' and hangs up.

Blasting the radio in his car and escaping from things till he gets there. But when he gets there, he's in for a surprise.

19

DON'T I KNOW YOU?

- - - - - - -

Light drizzle has started to fall, making the roads slippery, and the climb up through the Blue Mountains is a challenge at the best of times. Tragedy is not uncommon along this route, but thanks to the various areas of roadwork, it has slowed the traffic a little, making it harder for the lead-footed speed freaks to wreak havoc. As he climbs through Hartley, he can see the beautiful landscape, which has always made him feel pleasant and at peace. Mind you, that placid emotion doesn't stop his mind from thinking of new ways to kill and dispose.

Along the drive, he decides to drive into Katoomba and find a place for lunch. Parking is always an issue here with a myriad of tourists mixed with the locals. It takes a little while but he manages to find a spot. It was a good opportunity to scan the local fare and as a result he chooses the pie shop, 'Echo Pies-Est. 1954.' He just hopes the pies are fresh, fresh, fresh, fresh – imitating the sound of an echo – and smiles at the silliness of his joke. A little crowded inside, but the smell of freshly

baking pies and cakes is incredible. He was only peckish until now, and yet now, his tummy is grumbling and growling like a disgruntled lion.

With a couple of pies and a bottle of coke he wanders through the main street, sometimes stopping to look inside shop windows. A couple of old antique shops, and one in particular, has some old stuff his parents once owned, including a low-lying long buffet cupboard with glass sliding doors. He becomes bored very quickly, so decides to go back to his car and drive to Echo Point to check out the Three Sisters, and be lucky not to get the weekend crowds. Afterwards, and once he's happy with the view, he heads back to his car and continues on to Lithgow.

Not long now, and he will be pulling into the car park of the hotel, and hopefully, he can go in without really being noticed.

'Damn muddy car park, they still haven't filled those holes or stupid craters. I'm lucky I don't fall in and sink ten feet,' he mutters to himself, as he manoeuvres through and parks as far towards the back as he possibly can. Carefully, he climbs out of the car, trying to avoid the puddles scattered throughout the parking area and wanders to the rear entry of the hotel.

Inside it is quiet with a few patrons sitting on stools, drinking beer, and either chatting among themselves or watching the horse racing on the TV attached to the wall. He walks up to the bar, orders a beer and buys some nuts to go with it.

'Hey, do you have any accommodation available for tonight,' he asks the barmaid.

'Yeah, I think we do, I'll just check,' she replies. She is only gone for two minutes when she comes back with a room key and a registry book. She takes his name – Roger Donaldson – gives him a written receipt for the room, then goes back to wiping the bar over. With the keys in his hand, he walks over to a booth along the side of the room thinking how easy that was. A good position where he could sit and watch people without being too easily noticed. As there is little action and nothing really worth watching, he scans the area, hoping that someone has left a newspaper on a table – if he does not find one, he'll have to go without. The less he is seen, the better. As chance has it, there is a paper folded and stuffed between the seat and wall, just a few booths over, so he gets up and goes over to get it. 'Bugger, I need a pen,' he thinks, as he sits back in the booth.

He unravels the messy newspaper and goes pasty white. A photo of a girl he murdered three weeks ago has been found under a pile of leaves and branches. He could see a few fingers exposed under the debris, which was enough for her to be found. She is described in the usual fashion, 'Caucasian female, aged in her early twenties, with blunt force trauma to the back of her head. Some of her belongings were found several metres away and scattered throughout the area. Her identity has been withheld for the time being, until further investigations have been done. It is suspected that she was placed in the area after she was murdered, and the time of death is yet to be determined by the coroner.' He has seen a few bodies in the news over time, since he first started. The authorities have not connected the murders yet, but he senses that it's only a matter of time. This brings mixed emotions of happiness from seeing his work in the papers and a quiet nervous twitching inside, that one day, soon, his fun may be over.

Her name was Hannah, he remembers her well. What surprised him was how quickly she was found. He's not happy with having been a little sloppy this time round. As with just about every victim, there is likely no chance of them being on the police criminal database. So, while he removes all traces of identity, it should theoretically make it impossible to identify, short of dental records. Except that this time he was rushed and his tardiness may have him caught.

Only a matter of time.

Before winter sets in again, and while summer is still here he has to fulfil his murderous needs, and today is the day. If, he can find the right victim and right place. The time is always right, so once the rest falls into place, he can rest easy knowing that he won't have to worry about another victim until next summer. Until then, it's time to get some more nuts and another beer, and while he's at it, pick up one of those small pencils they use for the gambling game Keno. 'Never really good at crossword puzzles,' he mutters, and decides to give it a really good go.

Just as he is struggling with the puzzle, and actually getting frustrated, an argument breaks out between two guys, apparently over a gambling deal or something. It's only when one guy smashes a beer glass on the table and goes to attack his so-called mate, that he looks

up to see the fracas. Two bouncers come out of nowhere and calm the situation down, and just as he is about to turn back to his puzzle, he spies a young woman sitting at the bar texting, he guesses, on her phone. Probably waiting for a friend to arrive. Strangely she looks familiar, he just cannot recall why she is so. He sips his beer and thinks hard, but to no avail. So, he decides to let it go and go back to reading the newspaper. Something about the headline story fascinates him, and his intrigue makes him read the article thoroughly.

'Wait a minute,' he whispers. He looked back at the bar, but the young woman isn't there, she has moved to a table with stools and is chatting with a young guy, who may well have been her boyfriend, with that lovesick sparkle in his eyes. 'Surely she can't be . . .,' he says and pauses. It was distinctly possible that she is the girl that he saw running through the park when he came up to do that delivery only a few weeks ago. Though she is dressed a little too casual from how he remembers her, he is almost certainly sure she is the same girl.

His heart starts to race with excitement and his palms begin to get a little sweaty. As much as he had hoped he might find another victim, he had no idea just how lucky he was. If he could do this without a hitch, that might be the last, as summer winds down. He never really gave it any thought, until now, that practically every murder has happened in or near summer. It's his avid dislike of the colder weather that he has not committed his heinous crimes then.

After a few more beers and watching people coming and going, not at all surprised that any staff haven't come near him, he waits in anticipation of the young girl's next move. The guy that she has been drinking with left a few minutes ago, and she seems a little intoxicated. To avoid any suspicion, he gets up and walks back through the pub to the rear exit, and then makes his way around to the front corner, where he lights up a cigarette – always tastes better after a few beers – and waits. Night has fallen, and thankfully, there are no street lights that illuminate the area, and being dressed in dark clothing, he is quite inconspicuous. It feels like forever before she comes out, in fact, he thought, she may have left at the same time as he did and that she got a lift from someone. He cannot recall hearing the sound of a car driving away, so she must still be inside.

He stubs his cigarette under the foot of his Redstone steel cap boot, and is just about to walk past the pub, when she stumbles out, ever so gracefully, from the front door of the Highway Hotel. It is a quiet night and nobody seems to have noticed that she has left. She stands and pauses for a moment to gather herself, then turns and walks in his direction. He ducks back a little bit and waits until she has passed him, then counts to ten. It might sound silly but having tried this a few times to get some distance between him and his prey, it was an ideal count. He watches her walk up the road, once known as a highway, and to locals it still is – it is actually a two-lane bitumen road with a guttered edge alongside the hotel or pub, as he prefers to call it, and a gravel edge on the opposite side.

Here is where you will find about two kilometres of scrubby bushland that is yet to be sold for industry. A kilometre or so down the road, you will find a car yard selling cheap cars, 'We buy and sell your wheels, all cars under five thousand dollars.' Beyond that is a smash repairer, a motor mechanic and the Lithgow City Scrap Metal Yard. In the other direction, there are a few old colonial-style homes with wrap-around verandas and a post office that was built in 1839.

He follows her one block up, and picks up his pace, so he wouldn't lose sight of her. But just before doing so, he is able to quietly dash across the road and pick up a decent-sized rock, about the size of a baseball, then return to his stealthy movements until he is so close to her, he can smell a mix of alcohol and perfume. CRACK – across the back of her head, and she collapses immediately. It happens very quickly and she doesn't even get time to make a noise. At the end of the property he is standing beside, stands a small alleyway, so he picks her up and goes down about a hundred yards, where luck is on his side.

He stops right under a street light, but someone has smashed the globe, so he is gladly in the shade of night. A quiet moan alerts him to the fact that he has to finish business and now. He lays her on the ground in a position so that bashing her skull in would not leave any blood splatter on his clothes. He hits her once to knock her out, then takes her coat off and carefully lays it under her head. In doing so, he is able to achieve his goal and hopefully leave no trace of blood. The challenge now is how is he going to get rid of her. He cannot exactly just leave her lying in the alley, but definitely cannot be seen carrying her to the bushland. He has to get his car and come back for her, it's the only way.

His age is getting the better of him and he finds it harder to stand and straighten his back. Three houses down the back alley, he spots a dark tarp covering, what is possibly sand for a home renovation. 'Perfect coverage until I can get my car,' whispers Michael. He quickly goes down, quietly removes the four bricks holding the corners, and with the tarp and bricks in hand, he goes back to where she lays dead and covers her.

He takes a few moments to gather himself, draws a deep breath, pops his head out into the street to check that it's clear, then gracefully makes his way back to his car. The car park is almost empty and nobody is around to see him leave. However, no sooner did he pull out onto the main road and drive away, there are blue and red lights flashing in his rear-view mirror. After pulling over, it felt like forever before the police officer knocked on his window. The cop was doing a registration plate check and it was all good, naturally. Michael gives himself a quick check over for any bloodstains and is pleased that his efforts to stay clean have paid off.

Then panic sets in, he cannot remember how much he had to drink. Knowing that he was driving he had tried to keep it to one beer per hour, but he honestly cannot recall how much he consumed.

'Good evening, driver, got your licence there?' asks the officer. And as Michael was being asked, he was pulling his licence out of his faded and torn wallet. He'd been meaning to update it, but figured he'd get a new one for Christmas. 'Had anything to drink tonight?' he is asked.

'Yes, I have, about three in the last five hours. Last one about forty minutes ago,' says Michael.

'Count to ten in this device, please,' asks the cop.

'One, two, three, four, five, six, seven, eig—' and the cop pulls the breathalyser to check the read out.

There is a very long pause and Michael think he is gone. That would be the end of everything.

'Your lucky night, tonight. You are just under the limit,' explains the cop. 'Drive safe and have a good night,' the cop says, as he hands back Michael's licence. 'Oh, and your right tail light is out, though your brake light still comes on. Best get that fixed right away,' the officer says, just before he turns away and heads back to his Highway Patrol car.

Now, he has a Sydney address, and thinks that he can't go straight back to the laneway, that would look odd, so he acts quickly and says, 'Thanks, I'm staying at a mate's place up here tonight, so I don't have far to go. I'll get the light fixed first thing in the morning.' But already the officer is walking back to his patrol car. Naturally the cop sits and waits for Michael to drive away, but which way will he go? He tries his luck by driving two blocks up, and turns left, hoping that he can double back to the laneway to collect his prize. As Michael turns into the side street, the police car smoothly passes by, as it continues its hunt for lawbreakers.

For the first time, it feels like real pressure is upon him, because he still needs to dispose of the girl, and the place that he had in mind is now a little more of a hotspot. His car cannot be seen parked in an unusual place. Suddenly, he remembers that he can access Google Maps on his phone, and as such, he can investigate the layout of the land and search for a better place to get rid of her. Thank god for carrying a variety of tools.

About two kilometres away from the hotel, there is a fire trail so that is where he drives too. He has bolt cutters in case the gate is padlocked, but when he arrives, he discovers that the padlock has already been cut. He suspects it is the result of trail bike riders and he is grateful. Switching off his headlights and getting out of the car, he stops. Listening. The only sound he can hear is the incessant singing of cicadas. As quietly as he can, he opens the gate, goes back to his car, and drives a little way in, then gets out to close the gate. Slowly and cautiously, he drives without headlights, and drives until he can find a place he can easily walk through the thick trees – god! His back is aching tonight.

He pulls up a few hundred metres further in. He leaves the motor running, no need for anyone to hear a motor start up this time of night, and in such a remote area. He disposes of her in his usual fashion, with a lot of branches and twigs and leaves. What makes it easier for him, this time round, is that there is a dugout area. He can't make out why it's there and neither does he care – the noise of the cicadas is loud enough for him to snap branches and twigs to cover her completely. After what he'd read in the paper, and the fact that nobody knows that he is here, he has to make sure that she isn't found. He grabs her clutch bag and quickly checks inside for her identification, Anna-Maree, aged nineteen.

With that done, he closes the bag up and places it beside her. With a very thick covering of branches, twigs and leaves, he does one quick scan to satisfy himself, then turns to go. The wind starts to pick up a little bit and he can feel the sweat on his back, against his shirt, stick to him like glue. His eyes are stinging from droplets of sweat from his forehead, trickling downwards into his eyes, and running down his cheeks. It has to be the most refreshing feeling he's had in a while. Enough time wasted, he has to get going. He was told that the hotel locks its doors at 1:00 a.m., and right now it's a quarter to one. Post-haste, he makes his way back, and once upstairs, he showers before going to bed.

The following morning, he drives home feeling complete. Driving past the fire trail gate, he slows down to glance over the area and cannot see anything remotely disrupted there, it looks plain and as to be expected. Only one more week until summer is over, and he can relax for six months. Though, this won't stop him from seeing Jenny of course, because during this time he can talk with her about hypothetical scenarios, and ways of completing their devious tasks. His thirst has been quenched for now, and somehow, he's thankful. He feels somewhat exhausted, strange as it may sound, but it is the truth. He doubts he'd have the energy for one more killing. It is so mentally and physically draining, the way his whole body tenses up during the whole process, and it being towards the end of this summer – it had been the hottest summer recorded in nine years – damn El Niño affect.

In two hours, he is home. Louise is drinking – again – and it's not even midday yet, though close enough. The girls are at a friend's place; they were invited to go ice skating, and then have lunch with Michelle's best friend. The conversation is very light, no affectionate hugs or kisses when he got home either. 'What's with the scratches on your right arm?' asks Louise, in a very nonchalant manner.

'What? Oh, I had to park too close to a bunch of trees and scratched my arm up when I was undoing the chains on my truck,' he replies.

'Hmmm, looks nasty. Better get that cleaned up,' she says, as she gets up to go to the medicine cabinet above the stove in the kitchen.

He knows better than to argue the point with her and lets her fuss about. After all it's about the only affection he's had from her for a long time. 'There, feel better?' she enquiries.

'Much better. Thanks, Bub,' he says. The scratches undoubtedly came from when he was on the fire trail, the only light he had was the moon, and it wasn't a full moon either. With a lot of close trees and branches, he was unable to avoid the lower branches that were the cause of the minor abrasions. He suddenly thinks, 'Oh god, I didn't check to see if I've left a visible track snaking my way through the bush.' Well, naturally, there is nothing he can do now. Best let this go and move on. Winter is close by and hopefully it will get a good snow cover this year.

20

REBUILDING

- - - - - - -

inter provides a little more flexible time for Michael to spend with his family. He feels that the family structure is crumbling and nobody seems to have noticed or cared. Though he has this awful affliction and murderous desire, he truly does love his family. Michelle is turning eighteen soon, and he would really like to give her the best party that she has ever had. One to remember forever. However, with everyone barely on speaking terms, he must start to repair the cracks and strengthen the foundations. Louise is still drinking but has recently admitted this in private with Michael. She has asked him not to say anything to the girls, though he is almost certain that they know anyway. Louise started attending Alcoholics Anonymous (AA) meetings last month and though she has not yet stopped drinking, emotionally she is feeling better. To her amazement, they all supported her. Bobbie M has been going for twenty-three years, and still struggles, and as such through conversation, Louise nominated Bobbie M to be her sponsor.

Danielle has been in trouble with the police on a few occasions, though only minor criminal activity, with no charges laid. The police see her as a sensible young lady who is going through a difficult time and have given her a little slack. Now that she is almost sixteen, she has calmed down a little and mainly keeps to herself. She still wears the black Goth style clothing and black finger nail polish, something Michael doesn't really understand. However, lately, she has been a little chattier at home. A refreshing change from the dark and sinister mood so often noticed by her father more than anyone. He has thought on the odd occasion just how similar they are, when he is in a dark mood, it gets noticed and people just know to give him his space, and the same applies with Danielle.

Michelle has stopped seeing Wayne. Finally, the connection between her and the Whitsunday Island experience just got too much for her to deal with. Wayne was always moody and eventually she tired of supporting him and trying to keep him lifted up. She ended her time with him, six weeks ago, refusing to call it a relationship, and it is the best thing that she has done. It has allowed her to concentrate on her application for university next year. She has applied to two campuses so far, and is in the process of filling out an application for one more. Her interest is criminal forensics, and though this does concern Michael, he supports her one hundred percent.

The June long weekend is slowly approaching, and the family has not holidayed since Whitsunday. A three-day weekend is an ideal chance for them to get together and relax as a family. Hopefully, the plan will actually work, so tonight at dinner, he plans to discuss an option of going to Forster and staying at a caravan park. Sure, it might be cold but they can stay in a cabin and spend some quality time together, perhaps bring a board game or two. While he is at it, he can talk about what type of party Michelle wants.

'Dad, when we go to Forster, can we do some photography. We've been studying it at school and I kinda like it,' enquires Danielle. Michael is quite pleasantly surprised by her question.

'What a great idea, sweetheart. I haven't used my camera in a very long time so we could learn together,' replies her father. After dinner, Michael goes to the study and switches on the laptop to start some research into the long weekend. Meanwhile, as the computer slowly boots up, he goes to the fridge and grabs a cold beer, a little beef jerky from the pantry, and gives Louise a kiss on the cheek as he leaves to go back to the study. Closing the door behind him, he suddenly thinks of Jenny and wonders how she is coping on this horribly cold and windy night. He thinks about sending her an email but realises that it's probably not such a good idea for now. Though when he gets back from Forster, he will be keen as mustard to check his emails at work. Much to his dismay, almost all the accommodations are fully booked, and it looks like his idea may not go as planned, but he is determined to make this work. If his family fell apart completely, he would be doomed. With no idea how it would affect the serial killer within him, he could be worse, or totally the opposite and go into hiding. Regardless, he continues his search and a half hour later when it looks like he would come up empty, he discovers a little hideaway Bed and Breakfast that is perfect. It is described as a quite location, a five-minute drive from the town centre, and it can accommodate a family of four, with breakfast supplied. A lovely two-bedroom granny flat with beautiful gardens, pay TV, air conditioning which will provide warmth on the colder nights. A self-contained kitchen with a toaster, and coffee and tea available. This is perfect, so he sends an email to book the weekend, and makes sure he can secure this opportunity. He can pay for this with his credit card and is about do so when he notices the option for PayPal, and uses this method, as he feels it a more secure.

Michelle knocks on the study door just as her father closes the lid on the laptop and leans back in his office chair with his feet crossed at the ankles on the edge of the desk. 'Come in if ya good lookin,' he says, a favourite saying that makes his girls just shake their heads. Michelle thinks that she will never get used to her father's daddy jokes. 'What's up, baby girl? I thought you were going to bed early,' says Michael.

'Yeah, I was but came down to get a headache tablet, then thought I'd talk to you about my birthday party. I know you'd like to do something big, but all I really want is family. You know, just us and some cousins and stuff,' explains Michelle. 'Ok, darlin,' if that's what you want, we'll organise it for you. Write down the things you'd like at the party and your mother and I will make it happen.'

Michelle simply walks over and gives her father a huge hug, and whispers in his ear, 'I love you, Dad, you are the best father anyone could ask for.'

This brings a tear to his eye, and he says that he loves her more than life itself and is so proud of her. With that, she quietly leaves and goes back upstairs to her room to do some reading before going to sleep. Michelle's last words hit a cord with him and for the first time in his entire life, he feels sad and an unexpected level of guilt for the recent years of his horrid activities, his secrecy and lies. Finishing the last swallow of his beer – he desperately needs another – he gets up and goes into the kitchen to grab a couple of beers to take into the lounge room, where he decides to sit and catch up on the show Dexter. Louise has gone to bed with not so much as a good night, which is nothing new. So, with the family in bed, he has the house to himself. swinging his legs up, he stretches out on the lounge to blankly watch TV and contemplate his past, present and future.

Some time passes and his mobile phone buzzes silently in his pocket. His first thought is that his boss needs him for something, and almost ignores it, however, he is curious to find out who is messaging him this late at night. His face goes white and he nearly drops his beer. He sits, staring at the phone with disbelief, for what seems like an eternity. He reads the message a number of times, trying to understand it, when eventually, he replies by typing, 'How did you get my number?' The response comes back saying, 'I contacted your boss telling him that I was your sister and we haven't spoken in years and I'd lost your number.' Jenny was lonely and missed Michael's company, and knew that texting him was very risky, but she loved taking risks and knew that he did too. Michael hesitated for a short while, thinking what should he do, then he thinks that Louise never looks at his phone, and if he doesn't store her number, and deletes all her messages, then he's sweet. So, they text back and forth for the next hour or so before Michael calls it quits for the night and goes to bed.

Upstairs in his bedroom, Louise is lightly snoring, something that she claims she never does. He quietly undresses and climbs into bed and snuggles up to his wife, while thinking of his texting encounter with his murderous accomplice. Dreams come quickly and violently. Michael is being hunted through a deep forest by a group of men who hunt people for sport. He is running as fast as he can, jumping over huge trees that have fallen a long time ago, tripping over loose branches and stumbling a few times. Just when he thinks that he has lost the hunters, he finds himself surrounded by them. The lead hunter yells out to him, 'Where is Angelina?' Michael suddenly wakes up in a cold sweat crying out, 'I don't know! I don't know! I don't know!' This in turn wakes Louise, who is initially confused, until she realises that her husband has woken from a nightmare. She comforts him as best as she can, and Michael responds with gratitude by holding her tightly until his heart slows down and he catches his breath. Asking Michael what his dream was about, he ignorantly says that he cannot remember, something about work but cannot remember details. They both fall back asleep, Michael feeling uneasy but eventually drifting off, and sleeping soundly. The long weekend is coming soon and the break will be well deserved.

21

JENNY

As a young girl living in poverty, Jenny was always a mischievous tomboy, and forever getting into trouble. She would sometimes stay with her uncle John, though it was never her choice. He would molest her occasionally when the chance was there. Uncle John was her father's brother-in-law, married to Meagan. Together they had three children, all boys, and older than Jenny. Whenever Jenny stayed over and the house was empty, John would set upon Jenny with his devious intentions, threatening her that what he was doing wasn't wrong, but if she said anything then he would deny it. After all, she was the troublemaker in the family, and her parents would think that she was just being difficult as usual.

She didn't always go to school as she told her mum, instead she would steal her dad's cigarettes and go to the park to just hang out with a few friends from school. If she couldn't sneak food from the pantry at home, then she would steal from the local supermarket. She has been banned on a number of occasions but this has never bothered her.

Only once was she caught and taken to the police station. Her parents, though furious, felt that there was nothing that they could do but have a serious sit-down talk with her. To no avail as always, in one ear and out the other – blah, blah, blah. If things at home got really bad, she would lose her temper, maybe kick the dog on the way out of the house. She would run away for a couple of days and not tell anyone where she was. Once when she ran away, she killed a stray dog for trying to bite her. She had no remorse and no guilt. This would become a part of her nasty streak later in life.

Her childhood was one with very little genuine love and a lot of ignorance from most of her family. For no other reason than the fact that she never listened to anyone, nor took any helpful advice, instead, she felt that she knew enough to get her by, and that everyone else was in the wrong, that they had no idea of what they were talking about. She gained a reputation with the local police because of silly disrespectful antics when in public. Constantly escorted from the shopping centre because of her rowdy and noisy manner. School was different for her because for the times that she actually attended, it was an escape from home, and at times, reality. Sure, she was kicked out of class for daydreaming and simply not paying attention to the teacher, but remarkably never sent to the principal's office or suspended. She dropped out of high school early and got her first job as a coffee waitress, mainly serving coffee at a truck stop petrol station, about a half hour bus ride from home. Here, she worked long hours and earned a decent pay which she saved, as her goal was to move to Queensland and get away from her past forever. After three years in the job, it was time for a change but the trouble was, she had no experience doing anything other than serving customers. Luckily for her, the local paper had a small job vacancy section, and in that, Jenny found a Barista job in the city. Surry Hills is an arty suburb, with a lot of university students that attend The Sydney Monash University. Therefore, with a lot of younger people around, Jenny felt quite comfortable with this new job that would hopefully come with some benefits. It's there that she is introduced to marijuana, through a regular customer. He seemed a little too old to be studying at the university, but when she thought about it, nobody is too old to learn. Reuben came from a well-to-do family from Kensington, and his parents had been paying his tuition fees. For someone fairly comfortable, financially, his dressing sense was unusual. Holes in his denim jeans and a Slayer T-shirt, long greasy black hair and a nose piercing.

After several weeks of buying his short black double strength coffee, and after numerous conversations, he got the courage to ask her out to lunch. So, the following weekend they went for a seafood lunch in Darling Harbour, then went back to his city apartment to just chill and watch Netflix. This is when he pulled out his fancy bong and a bowl with weed and tobacco in it. She looked in amazement at his calmness and carefree attitude, as he sat and packed the bong, then lit it, drew back, held it in and then blew the smoke out. Suddenly glassy eyed, he turned and asked her if she wanted a hit.

At first, she was about to say no but thought, 'Fuck it, you only live once.' So, he packed her a hit and she gave it the best she could, a little cough at first, but managed herself quite well. Several more bongs and it seemed irrelevant what was on TV, they just sat and chatted about nothing.

Several hours had passed and they fell asleep in the lounge room, but it was what happened in the morning that changed her life forever. She woke to find Reuben having sex with her, she'd been asleep and he thought he'd take advantage of her. Big mistake because she thought at first that it was her Uncle again and totally flipped out. After she struggled to push him off, she jumped up and ran to the kitchen. Thankfully, he was quite untidy and had lots of utensils splayed across the benchtop, and she grabbed the biggest knife and sternly headed back to the lounge room. He was just sitting there as if nothing had happened, and just as calmly as he packed the bong, she plunged the knife into the side of his neck, right into the jugular vein. That was the first of thirty-seven stab wounds that ended his life.

She left Sydney that very moment and moved to Wollongong, into a granny flat under a different name. For a few days, she just sat on the beach in a haze of depression and hate. She barely ate, though she did manage to keep her hygiene up. She did not speak to anyone for a week until she began to settle into what felt like normal. On a sunny weekend, she decided to buy a hamburger to have in the park for lunch, and on her way there, she happened to walk past a coffee shop and in the window, there was a small advertisement for a casual part-time Barista. So naturally, she applied because money doesn't grow on trees, and she was getting short on cash. The next day, she went back to check out whether or not she got the job – she had gotten it – she started that afternoon. This was to be her quite life for the next few years, before eventually moving back to Sydney, and eventually meeting Michael.

22

THE LONG WEEKEND

- - - - - - -

Leaving their home behind on a late Thursday afternoon, the family headed north for a long weekend, so that they could take a brief moment away from their busy life to unwind. The trip took just over three hours, and thankfully, the traffic was not too heavy, and with a late check-in, they settled in for the evening rather quickly.

Michael found the TV remote and switched the TV on to see what shows were on. Louise put the kettle on to make coffee, and the girls sat quietly on the two-seater lounge in the motel room, reading through the visitor brochures.

'Ok, guys, breakfast is ready,' shouts Louise from the little kitchen window in their holiday cabin in Coffs Harbour. Michael is on the front steps enjoying the warmth from the sun reading the local paper, while the girls are out taking photos of flowers in the garden. Slowly they drift in and sit quietly, enjoying bacon and eggs, with juice for the girls, coffee for Michael and tea for Louise. In the quiet, Michelle asks what they are going to do today, and her dad says that they are going to

Dolphin World. Both girls roll their eyes in a manner of boredom, but reply with a false enthusiasm that Michael picks up but ignores.

After breakfast, they leave to go and see the dolphins, and the girls are grumbling under their breath. It's clear that this weekend isn't doing what Michael had hoped, though it's not over yet. Danielle brought her camera and she is so glad that she did, as she thinks that she has gotten some incredible photos. Along with watching the dolphins swimming and doing their jumps and flips, there was also a seal show. The usual ball balancing tricks and fish feeding. What Michelle had not expected, and which gave them all the biggest belly laugh was, a seal had wiggled up to her and gave her a BIG, smelly, wet kiss.

That seemed to be the magic that broke the angst hidden within the family. They all then had lunch at the cafeteria before a little sightseeing. Both Michael and Danielle have been taking plenty of photos and while they are sharing ideas, Louise and Michelle bond a little more than they have in what must be almost a year. Before leaving the Dolphin Park, they did a little browsing inside the gift shop. Michael bought himself an extra-large T-shirt for wearing around the house, to mow the lawns in or work on the car. Louise and Michelle each buy a bookmark as a memento, and Danielle, well, she doesn't find anything that she likes, so goes out empty-handed.

The weather is starting to take a turn with dark luminous clouds building, so they make their way to the car for the short drive back to the small motel room, where it will be safe and dry. As they are getting close, Louise asks if they can stop by the grocery store to grab some snacks for after dinner, and everyone agrees that it was a great idea. The grocery store is close by the waterfront and Danielle sees a perfect opportunity for some quick shots. The dark clouds in the sky along with very light rain and a very large coloured rainbow make for an award-winning photo, one that she hopes will be good enough to frame.

That night they go to the local pizza store and order a few to take back to their room, and after dinner, Michael surprises them with a game called Mouthguard. The concept is that a person wears a mouthguard so that the mouth is constantly open, then must read out a word or a phrase, and everyone else has to guess what the player is trying to say. It causes hysterics and they laugh so hard that tears fall down their cheeks. They play for about an hour, that's all they could deal with, their jaws were aching. So, the girls turn in for the night, and both Michael and Louise sit up for some time, talking. Louise feels that it was time to talk to the girls about her drinking, but Michael disagrees stating that, finally, there is some happiness within the family unit, and this could just send things backwards. With careful thought, Louise sees the sense in Michael's suggestion to leave it for a little while longer.

What neither of them know yet is that Louise will be forced to give up drinking.

Sunday morning, they wake to a bright sunny day, which surprises them after last night's nasty and very loud thunderstorm. The thunder was so bad at times, the windows rattled. Again, Louise cooks up a fantastic breakfast with bacon, eggs, and this time, fried tomatoes. After which, the girls insist on washing the breakfast dishes.

'Ok, who stole my daughters?' asks Michael. 'I mean it, I want them back. Who are these imposters?' he exclaims. Louise replies in kind and the girls giggle. Michelle says that the daughters were kidnapped last night and they were the replacements. This brought light laughter to the morning and a great start to the day. Thanks to the beautiful weather, Michael's plan for the day could go ahead. At Seven Mile Beach, there is a National Park where they can walk and be at one with nature. The smell of the ocean and the sound of birds singing in the trees, life couldn't be better. When they arrive, Danielle rushes out of the car, camera in hand, and starts to discover the beautiful flora near the entrance to the walk. Getting down on her knees to capture some pretty purple and blue flowers. The rest of the family catch up and then begin their slow walk through the national park. They see a tree snake about ten minutes into their walk, and though it seemed a little scary, he was quite high up in the tree, and therefore out of harm's way. Danielle keeps falling behind because she has become addicted to taking photos, and suddenly everything fascinates her. Her father knows what it means to be addicted to something, and when Louise seemed a little short towards Danielle, he calmly said that she wasn't hurting anyone, and she couldn't get lost on the trail. Louise guesses that she is a little agitated because she has not had anything to drink over the weekend, and so, desperately wants one.

They take about an hour or so on their walk and when they get back to the car, Louise has some bread rolls for lunch. She made them the night before after the girls went to sleep, so Michelle gets the picnic blanket from the boot of the car, while Danielle gets the basket of goodies. Michael packed a small cooler bag with soft drinks in it and a little surprise for his wife. The sun was high and the breeze was light, so Michael suggested that they go down onto the beach and have some lunch. 'Danielle, I want you to leave your camera in the car. I don't think it's a good idea having it on the sand. Put it on the floor behind my seat, please,' says Michael.

'Ok, Daddy, but wait for me,' replies Danielle. With the blanket laid out, the girls wearing hats to keep the sun off their faces – their mum hands out the bread rolls and Michael hands out the drinks. 'Hey, Bub, I have a little surprise for you. Close your eyes,' he says. Her hands held out and eyes tightly closed, he hands her a small bottle of wine from the bar fridge in their room. She has shown great restraint by not touching anything from the bar fridge, so though he knows she has a problem, he wants her to enjoy the weekend as well. To him it's about reward and family bonding. 'OH MY GOD! You are simply the best husband ever. Thank you. What made you do this?' she shyly asks.

'I have to drive so I cannot drink, but you can. You have been a great mum and wife, so a little thank you is in order,' says Michael. The girls DO know that their mum drinks more than she should and are, at first, puzzled about this. But when their father says that a little thank you is in order, they cannot argue with that. Mum has been really easy to get along with this weekend, despite no drinking, and believe that just one can't hurt. They were right too, it loosened Louise up a little and her mood seemed a little bit happier again.

After lunch, Michael insists that he clean up, and takes everything to the car while the three ladies walk along the foreshore, wetting their feet and collecting shells. 'Hey, Mum, have a look at this weird shaped sh— AARRGGGH,' screams Michelle. She had picked up a hermit crab shell that still had a live crab living in it. Out of character, it popped its little claw out scaring Michelle. Danielle came rushing over to see wishing that she had her camera. Mum wandered over and saw the shell, saying how cool it looked and as she was saying that, it started to crawl away.

After thirty minutes of walking on the beach, and with the wind picking up, it was time to go back to the car. Then back to the motel room for dinner. No games that night, as they were all more tired than they had expected to be.

'What a great weekend. Hun, you are amazing. You organised all of this and I think I can speak for the girls as well that it was the best holiday ever,' says Louise.

'Yep, sure was,' both girls said at the exact same time, again. This always made Michael smile, but this time, the smile was bigger, because not only did the girls speak in unison, but because his plan had worked. The peace and happiness were back.

Now just to keep it going.

23

TRAGEDY

- - - - - - -

Michael took the Monday of work, so that he could drive the family home without the congestion of the long weekend traffic. An early rise on Monday morning with a quick breakfast of toast and coffee, cereal and juice for the girls and a cup of tea for Louise – a good start to the day with light chatter and smiles all round.

At first, the traffic was really heavy heading out towards the freeway, and it seemed to have no end. The drive should have taken around ten minutes to get to the freeway. However, due to a truck breakdown that blocked one lane, the drive took thirty-seven minutes.

The local radio station had a traffic report with regular updates, but that didn't cool Michael's seething temper, quietly hidden though Danielle picked up on it. She told her dad that she really had a great weekend and that she loved him with all her heart. This softened him enough to lighten his mood, and as he began to feel a little better. A song came on the radio that got everyone singing. Before he knew it, they were on the freeway and on their way home – huge trucks in the left lane were left behind in the rear-view mirror. Naturally, the freeway traffic was without incident, but that was short-lived once they reached the fringes of Sydney – if you have ever driven along Pennant Hills Road, you'll know just how congested and crazy the traffic can be. The traffic eased up once they passed the Castle Hill turn off, and this is where Michael's concentration slackened off. His mind started to wander, and he began to think about the workload ahead of him at work, and how he was looking forward to getting back on the computer and touching base with Jenny. BANG – suddenly a speeding car being chased by the police, comes racing out of a side street and smashes into the rear left-hand side of the family car. The car goes spinning off in a forward to right direction, slamming into a tree. The car is a mess, with broken glass everywhere, and barely recognisable, everyone unconscious. A crowd has quickly gathered around the wreckage with people trying to get the family out. The left side of the car is pushed in too far and the doors are jammed, so, Jacko races around to the other side and is able to open the back door. The young girls are covered in blood, with glass fragments in their faces. The seat belts are jammed and won't open either, so Jacko yells out, 'Does anyone have any blankets? We need to keep them warm until rescue gets here.' The rescue team arrives within minutes, and shortly thereafter, Louise regains consciousness in a panic. She is trapped in the wreckage and cannot move, so begins yelling out to her girls and Michael, but with no answer – panic sets in. Barely consciousness, Louise is finally cut free and transported to the Royal North Shore Hospital, where she immediately goes into surgery for internal injuries and a shattered collarbone.

Michael had to be cut out of the car as it was his door that had hit the tree and had trapped him behind the steering wheel. With cuts and abrasions, plus a broken wrist, he never felt any pain due to floating in and out of consciousness. He is sent straight to the emergency operating room for treatment, where afterwards, he is placed in intensive care. With damaged organs, he is placed into an induced coma for a period of two weeks to allow his body to heal. At the crash scene, Danielle is pronounced dead at the scene. She took the full brunt of the force of the accident and there was no way to have avoided it. Michelle was also transported to the hospital with minor injuries and is kept overnight for observation. A crash scene is set up to investigate the accident, and it would be months before anything went to court. The case would go on for months and it would seem as though the offending driver would not be convicted. Or would he . . . Three days later, Louise is released from hospital and goes to her sister's place to pick up Michelle. On her way, she goes over in her mind, at least a hundred times, how she was going to tell her daughter that her sister died in the car accident. Her heart feels as heavy as lead, beads of sweat slowly falling from her forehead. Tears cascade down her cheeks with such a broken heart, and she still doesn't even know if Michael will come out of the coma. How will she ever go on?

Slowly pulling into the driveway, she draws a deep breath and finds the strength to compose herself, wiping away the tears. Just as she is opening the car door, Michelle is running towards the car yelling out, 'Mummy!' Michelle was sitting on the front steps to get some fresh air and a little alone time, and wasn't expecting her mother until the following day, so this was the best surprise ever.

Louise's Sister Rhonda comes out hearing a small commotion and walked over to embrace her. They both hug in silence and then go inside. Rhonda puts the jug on to make tea and puts some biscuits on a plate for everyone. Michelle settles for juice and is quite solemn. The silence seems to last forever, when finally, Michelle asks about Danielle. She could see the sadness on her mum's face and the tears that are beginning to form. Nothing had to be said to Michelle to understand the reality of the situation, she somehow felt it in her soul that her sister was gone. 'It's ok, mum, you don't have to say anything. I know, I can feel it.'

Then Louise spoke, with a crackly broken voice, 'Danielle was killed instantly and we can be grateful that she wasn't in pain at all. Dad is still in a coma and we won't know for a while how will he be. The doctors are keeping a close eye on him. We can go and visit him tomorrow if you'd like?'

The three sit and quietly speak for the next few hours before Louise and Michelle go home – home, empty and eerie. They both sleep poorly that night but manage to sleep in their own beds. The next morning is the hardest of all as the house has this strange emptiness about it. No attitude from Danielle, or Michael telling the girls to keep it down as it's too early in the morning for him. They arrive at the hospital around ten that morning and go straight to Michael's bedside. It is so hard for both of them to look at him with hoses and tubes everywhere, plus a breathing apparatus to breathe for him. It did not look promising at all. They kept up this vigil for the next two months until the doctors deem it time to bring Michael out of the coma.

Every week they did a variety of tests, including taking blood. At one stage, his organs looked to be deteriorating, however, into the second week of Michael's induced coma, the test results were beginning to look very positive. Yes, he definitely was a fighter, and in the end, it was the only thing that really saved him from the near fatal accident. The one that killed his daughter and changed his life for the better. Early Tuesday morning, with Louise and Michelle sitting beside his bed, like they had for the last two weeks, seemed just like another ordinary start to their day.

What happened next surprised Louise more than Michelle.

'Where am I? Who are you? What's going on?'

Amnesia.

A meeting was held with Louise and her daughter to explain that what Michael was experiencing is temporary amnesia. How much he will remember, and how soon things will come back to him, they cannot say. Time is on their side, and with support and patience, Michael should remember most things. Strangely though, he cannot remember anything at all from before the accident. Yes, he remembers his family and most parts of his job, but other than that, he draws a blank.

It took six months before the doctors gave Michael the all clear to go back to work. It scared the hell out of him and he was reluctant at first to go back. He knew that there would be a lot of questions and also a lot of sympathy. Neither of which he wanted to face. The first day back, his office desk was filled with flowers and cards from all the staff. What surprised him more was the support from everyone, nobody asked him uncomfortable or awkward questions, only asked if he wanted coffee. They tried to make his day feel like any other, with the usual shit they face every day.

The first week was far harder than he expected, even though he knew it wouldn't be easy. So, he arranged a meeting with Jordan to discuss his duties and roster, as he felt that three days a week will be more beneficial to both himself and the company. Jonathon Myers filled in for Michael while he was in the hospital, he also worked in the office, though he was more involved in the purchasing side of the business, and he also helped Michael when it was needed. Jonathon was more than happy with the change of scenery, and so when asked if he could help out for a little while longer, he didn't hesitate. Michael received an email from someone called Jenny – he doesn't know any Jenny. Apparently, she knows him and was asking strange questions about catching up again, to taking up where they left off. He hesitated at first, fingers poised over the keyboard wondering if he should reply. Then simply replied that he had been off work due to ill health, had no idea who she was and asked her not to contact him again, hoping that was the end of it. Meanwhile, behind the scenes and unbeknownst to Michael, there was something in the background that would have him questioning his whole life.

24

WHO AM I?

- - - - - - -

Dozens of people go missing each year, some never to be seen again. It's never known if they assume a new identity and travel to new and interesting places, or are murdered and their bodies are hidden or dumped in strange far off areas, like the scrub or the bushland. Long gone are the days when you would see a missing person's poster in a shop window, or on a milk carton. Rarely do you see anyone handing out flyers asking if this person has been seen in the area. It's hardly even a big enough story to make the 6:00 a.m. news, unless it's associated with a high society member.

So, when the police come knocking on Michael's door, he has not a clue what they are talking about. He cannot even remember being questioned about a body found deceased on a delivery route he used to do for work. To make things more confusing, the police ask if he has ever heard of a person called Hannah. Naturally, given his amnesia, he has no recollection of the name and admits he has never heard of this person. A KVT truck was seen in the area that she went missing, though the police refrain from saying where she was found. All drivers are being questioned, and he is told that if he remembers anything at all, to notify the police immediately. Fat chance of that happening but he tells them that if something comes to mind, he'll call right away. That night he sits with Louise at the dining table very soberly, with a cold beer, while Louise sips on green tea. Since the accident, she has not touched a drop of alcohol and refuses to ever again. Michelle is now a hermit at home, barely coming out of her room, so it's a pleasant surprise to see her walk in the room. 'Mum, can I have some juice?' she quietly asks, before going to the fridge. Then she joins her parents at the table.

The house has never felt so empty and the silence is deafening. No one really knows what to say without talking about Danielle, yet they all need to say SOMETHING. Moments go by, when Michelle says, 'I miss her.' Louise turns her head away slightly to hide the tears slowly falling down her red cheeks, and to cover her puffy eyes. Crying seems to be all that she can do. With a shaky voice which concerns Michael, she replies, 'We all do, Hun, we should never have gone on that holiday.' As she says this, she turns to look at Michael as if he was to blame, and the sadness in her eyes tells the whole story.

Feeling defenceless, Michael gets up and walks away. Unsure of what he will do next, he finds himself walking towards Danielle's room. Since her death, nobody goes into her room. As soon as Louise had a chance, and while Michael was still in the induced coma, she made Danielle's bedroom a shrine. With a small table in one corner, which displays with candles, the remainder of the room lays untouched. On the walls are posters of the bands that Danielle liked, which Michael never really liked. All that grunge, or whatever she called it. A huge poster of some guy called Kurt Cobain hangs directly above her pillow, and smaller pictures scattered around, gives the room a dark and melancholy feel. Unknowingly, he sits on her bed feeling totally numb. He feels like he is in some kind of a weird trance, like it is all a dream. Looking around to try and find some normality in this madness, he reaches across to her bed side table and opens the drawer. Staring at the drawer for only a moment, he notices a diary. 'I had no idea Dani kept a diary. Though I guess it's a typical teenage girl kinda thing to do,' he whispers to the room.

He flicks through random pages, not meaning to find anything in particular, until he comes to a page with a big upside cross in heavy black ink. He starts reading it with complete confusion, as what he is reading does not make sense. She is describing a man who has killed a small dog and buried it in the backyard. Danielle says that it was her father who was the murderer and that she suspects that it's not the first time he's done something like this.

Stunned.

He is in complete shock. Sure, he is suffering from amnesia and some memory loss is to be expected. However, he now questions just what kind of person he was before the accident. Surely, he didn't mastermind the accident which caused his daughter's death. Then again, if he killed a dog in secrecy, could it be possible? He can't ask anyone either, that would raise too many questions. Questions he doesn't think he wants asked, because then there would be answers, and that is something he doesn't want to know.

Is that what the police were talking about when they were questioning him? So much is going through his head, and his head is spinning almost out of control. He closes his eyes to try to gain some composure in his surroundings – a knock on the door surprises him, and he quickly stands just as the door opens, and hides the diary behind his back.

'What are you doing in here?' asks Louise.

Michael drops his head and says, 'I don't know, babe. I guess I needed to feel that this is real and not some horrible nightmare. I was in a coma and didn't get to say goodbye to my daughter, and there is this big empty space inside of me. Being in here feels right. Let's light some candles and pray that god is watching over her.'

Louise agrees but needs to get a lighter or some matches, forgetting that Michael smokes and should be carrying a lighter. This new situation can make it easy to forget some of the basic and simple things. This gives Michael a chance to hide the diary, but for now, he places it in the small of his back, inside his jeans, until he can find a safe place, perhaps in the garage.

Louise calls Michelle and tells her that she is wanted upstairs. A minute or so later, Michelle wandered towards her sister's room and freezes in her tracks. 'I can't go in there, Mum, I just can't.' Her father says to her that they both understand, but could she at least stand at the door as they say a little prayer. Reluctantly, Michelle does stand at the door and without realising it, she finds herself standing beside her mum in Danielle's room. They all say a prayer and thank the Lord for watching over their angel. After a minute's silence, both the women go back downstairs, where Louise puts the jug on to make a cup of Chamomile tea for herself and hot chocolate for Michelle. Michael says he would be down in a few minutes – this allows him time to focus on where he will hide the diary for future retrieval.

It was decided that every Sunday morning, they would all gather together for prayer in Danielle's room, to show their respects. A ritual that they will never stop doing, regardless of what the future holds.

The following morning, Louise goes to the supermarket to pick up essential groceries, and perhaps, while she is out, pick up some fresh flowers for the dining table. The home is looking a little drab, and a splash of fragrance and colour is just what it needs. Michelle left for school early as she has an exam for her English class, and for which she has done little study, so she plans on going to the library before class, and do some cramming before the test. Michael called in sick, stating that he has a migraine and not up to coming in. Of course, considering what he has been through, Jordan has no problem with this, and even suggests taking tomorrow off as it is a little quiet at the moment. After his daughter and wife went to bed last night, Michael decided to stay up and watch a movie on TV, something about an off-duty policeman in winter, fighting some terrorists. This gave him time to store the diary, which is now hidden behind the DVD player in the TV cabinet. Now, with the house to himself, he makes a coffee and then retrieves this intriguing book to read a number of times. He is still in disbelief that it's about him.

Before taking time to make a sandwich for lunch, he needs some fresh air. All that reading has made him feel closed in and he needs some fresh air. A block from his home is a corner petrol station, so he wanders in to buy a cold bottle of water. The warmth of the day has made him thirsty. As he approaches the counter to pay for his beverage, he glances to his right where the daily paper is being sold. The front-page story tells of a fourth body found with a similar MO, and the fact that there may be links to others. The police suspect that a serial killer is responsible for these deaths. He picks up a copy to take home and read more about this awful news.

25

FINDING OUT

The head of police has called a meeting with Task Force Hammerhead to brief the team on new information regarding the case. Chief Inspector Harrison started this Task Force nearly a year ago after the third body was found, and the results from the Coroner confirmed the nature of each death – if not the same, very similar. Blunt force trauma to the skull, usually at the back of the skull. This fourth body again has the same MO, and it is worrying to the police force that there may be more bodies out there. The trouble with the case is the lack of evidence, except for cigarette butts near or close by to where the bodies were found. No weapons have been found either. DNA testing has been done with no results, no hits on the database, and no fingerprints have been found on these butts, leaving a dead end. The idea of publishing this information in the newspaper is in strong debate; the fear of panic within the community is of great concern. Not to mention the nature of information given – not even a sketch of any possible suspect. So, it's decided that for the next week or two, it is kept out of the tabloids.

Chief Inspector Harrison announces to everyone in attendance that this needs to be kept under wraps until further notice. 'Constable Erickson will be leading the charge in bringing this case to a close. If you have any information at all, anything, as little as it may seem can help, please see Constable Erickson. We will meet again on Thursday to review this case.'

The following day, after the meeting, Constable Erickson pays another visit to KRT Transport to talk with Michael. There seems to be something that doesn't feel right about him.

'Hi Michael, Jordan has allowed me ten minutes alone with you, I hope you don't mind?' says the police officer.

'Not at all, always happy to chat. What is this about?' enquires Michael.

'Earlier in the year I spoke with you in regards to your fellow worker Frank Spiteri. Also, we spoke about the incident on the Princess Highway heading towards Batemans Bay, do you remember anything from that delivery that day? Did you see anything or anyone that looked out of place?'

'I really wish I could help you officer, but after my car accident a few months ago, I cannot remember anything from before then. I have basically no recollection of Frank at all, but I was told a little about the accident. Apparently, it happened on a fishing trip, but I don't ever remember going fishing with anyone on a boat,' he explains.

'The information I recall was that you and your work colleagues went out on a deep-sea fishing boat, and the water got choppy when Frank was stabbed to death with your knife. It was recorded as an accident for the courts and the forensic evidence backed it up,' says the officer.

'I don't like the tone of your voice, mate, are you implying that I had something to do with the accident?' Michael asks with tension in his voice.

'Not at all. Also, there is the incident with the deceased body found in an area where a delivery docket was found with the company logo. This was southbound heading towards Batemans Bay. I have spoken to Jordan who says that you were the driver for that delivery run,' says Erickson.

'Sorry, officer, I can't help you there. If the paperwork says I was out that way on the said day, then I was out that way, but like I said, I don't remember anything before my accident,' replies Michael.

Constable Erickson thinks to himself how convenient it is to forget everything before the car accident. He jots down in his pocket notebook to check with the hospital medical records to see if Michael's story is correct. As for the other information regarding the recent findings of other victims, he will leave it alone until he's spoken with the doctors. 'Sorry to have taken up your time, if you do happen to remember anything, no matter how small, please call me,' he says as he hands Michael his business card.

The officer shakes Michael's hand and says nothing as he walks back to his car, but looks back just once to try and read any body language that might give him a sense of Michael hiding something. Like a stone, Michael has no expression on his face, and stands upright with his shoulders back, sternly.

Michael goes back to his desk duties until it's time to leave work. Shortly after getting back to his desk, a bleep alarm sounds indicating that he has a new email. Someone named Jenny Moore. He has seen this name before but cannot remember where. Since his accident, this person has sent a few emails, and each time he ignores them. This time, the heading, 'Let's meet for murder,' sends chills throughout his body. Given the diary that he found in his daughter's bedroom, and the visit by that arrogant cop, he is almost afraid to open it, yet finds he can't help himself. Even as he is telling himself to ignore he finds himself clicking on the email and opening it.

'Dear Michael,

I have been very worried about you. I know that you said to keep our relationship secret and not to contact you at work, but after not hearing from you for three months, I had to ring your work. I spoke to your boss but can't remember his name, Gordon, I think it is. Anyway, I said that I was a cousin and wanted to know if there was anything wrong and he told me that you had been in a coma from a bad car accident. I am not even sure you are back at work yet but hope that if you are, that you are getting better.

When we last caught up we were talking about our little team effort on killing people, you had someone in mind and I have the bug really bad. I know you have your own methods and I've learned a lot from you. I want to meet up again soon to talk more about US. I miss you and the time we spent together.

Write back soon.

Love, Jenny.'

Michael slumps in his chair, as he's reading this with absolute disbelief. He cannot begin to imagine what he has supposedly done. He quickly closes the email then runs to the toilet to vomit. He feels sick to the stomach and weak to the knees. Is it really possible that he really is a monster? And who is this Jenny? Was he having an affair with her and if so, how long?

He is now at a loss for what to do from here. He tells Jordan that he is feeling unwell and says he is going home, and Jordan claims that Michael is looking pale. 'Did you get most of your work caught up on, Mike?'

'Yeah, boss, the rest can wait 'til tomorrow.'

So, he sits in his car for a few minutes to compose himself before driving home. When he gets there, he'll just tell Louise that he's ok, just a little off. While he is driving home, all these images crash and bump into each other flooding his mind with dark and disturbing thoughts. He just cannot believe that he's capable of murder. He actually feels numb and like he is floating on air, the shock of today is really weighing heavily on him.

Officer Erickson is already at his home before he gets there, and as he pulls into his driveway, he is suddenly filled with rage, uncontrollable rage. He storms into his house and starts up in the officer's face, 'I told you I don't fucking know anything, now get the fuck out of my house unless you have a search warrant. Do not come back unless you have a warrant and leave my fucking family alone.'

Louise stands there in complete shock. She has never seen her husband so mad before, sure he'd get cranky sometimes, we all do, but this is scary. The officer tries to calm Michael down by explaining that he is here just asking routine questions about missing cases. Michael then takes a deep breath to gather himself, then politely tells Officer Erickson that he has no further information to give and that he should leave.

The officer obliges and leaves, but before doing so, he leaves a business card with Louise and asks her to contact him if anything comes up during conversation. As the police officer walks out of the front door, Michael follows closely behind him, making sure that he leaves, slamming the front door behind him.

'MICHAEL! What has gotten into you? That's not like you to get so mad. What is your problem?'

'That arsehole pig harassed me at work claiming that I was responsible for Frank's death, plus some stupid story of me being involved in a murdered girl down south,' he replies, as he slows his breathing.

'But we all know Frank's death was an accident. And what girl is he talking about?' she asks.

'I don't know. Something about a body found on a route I did a delivery on, heading towards Batemans Bay. But like I told him, I don't remember anything from before the accident. I don't even recall any of the deliveries that I am supposed to have done. I'm going out the back to sit and try and calm down, I am sorry, Hun, that I got so mad. I didn't think I had it in me and won't explode like that again,' he says.

Firstly, he walks out to his garage where his fridge is stocked with beer and where he secretly keeps his daughter's diary. After getting a beer and the diary, he goes out the back and starts to read the diary again. The feeling of floating and numbness creeps back in. Then out of nowhere, he remembers that daunting email and begs the question of reality. He needs to seriously consider his next move, as he knows that prick cop will be back with more questions.

'Perhaps it's time to reply to, what's her name . . . oh, yeah, Jenny. Maybe she can fill in some blanks. But how and when?'

26

THE CALL

- - - - - - -

Four days after the officer was asked to leave Michael's house, the Task Force has gathered more intel. Another body has been found, this time on a fire trail in Lithgow. Tyre tracks were too badly worn to determine the type of vehicle, however, a cigarette butt was found close to the body. The MO appears to be the same as the others, with blunt force trauma to the head, so now, a plan needs to be put in place to get the suspect's DNA. Knowing that the suspect will not be willing to just give a sample to the investigating police force, it is decided to arrange a meeting to discuss the case with this person of interest.

Meanwhile, Michael has replied to the email and is meeting up with Jenny that afternoon. He needs to get this sorted out so that he knows what he is up against, the next time the cops decide to pay another visit. The old motel looks unfamiliar to him as does Jenny. It is only when she calls out to him and goes running to him that he knows that he has the right person. He has a look of bewilderment as she approaches, and this slows her approach, suddenly cautious of him. It's not a good look on him, and suddenly she is not sure if this was a good idea.

'Jenny? Is that you? Hi, there. Sorry if I startled you, I just don't remember you,' says Michael.

'Hi, babe, it's ok. I have a room booked where we can be alone to talk. Follow me.'

As they approach the room, Michael feels uncomfortable, like someone is watching them. Though this feeling subsides, he can't quite shake it. Just the same, he goes into the room and closes the door behind him. Jenny gets a beer from the fridge and pours herself a scotch, then sits to begin their overdue catch up. She explains in vivid detail their past interactions, including her story and the amazing sex they had. She also fills in all the blanks regarding Michael's part in the murders before they met. Michael sits in silence and is as white as a ghost. They both sit in silence for what feels like eternity. He finally breaks the silence by asking her how long had this been going on, before the accident, and all she can say is that she has only known him for close to twelve months. Before that, judging from what Michael had told her, whether or not she believed him, she told him as far as she knew, it had been quite a few years.

Jenny seems quite unsure of this meeting now, as before this meeting she had total trust in him. Now, she feels on edge and suddenly worried that Michael may do something that they will both regret. Though to be perfectly honest, she really doesn't care about Michael anymore. It's her life she needs to be concerned about. And she will not go to jail for anyone. This sudden turn of events has made her feel that he is just another useless male that has let her down. She needs to think carefully about everything that she says or does around Michael.

'I am sorry if this has come as a shock to you. I figured that you would remember at least something from your past. What will you do now?' asks Jenny.

'One thing is for sure, Jen, I need to lay low and stay quiet. I need time to process this information. I just can't believe that I am capable of anything like this,' he replies. Michael isn't even sure that he can go home now and face his wife.

Meanwhile, across the road, there is a surveillance van recording their conversation. Neither are even aware of the microphone hidden under the dining table. Chief Inspector Harrison, in conjunction with Task Force Hammerhead, have been following Michael for a while, including his emails and phone calls. They are only gathering evidence for now but want to catch him in the act. They are after both Jenny and Michael, but want to use Jenny as bait. Once the pair have finished meeting up and part ways, the detectives clean the room, collecting the empty beer bottles and the scotch glass for forensic evidence. The Task Force has been busy gathering information, some of which did not come easily. Checking the bank records of Jenny did not indicate any financial gain from Michael or their endeavours, however, it was able to provide them with an address for Jenny, so the police are on the hunt now to interview her about the murders.

The following day, Senior Constable Oscar Fields and Constable Erickson pay a visit to the home of Jenny Russo. They speak briefly with her before escorting her to Strathfield Police Station for further questioning. Initially, Jenny does not have much to say about her knowledge of Michael, or any interaction with him, and keeps this going for over an hour. When the officers tell her of the meeting a few days ago at the Oasis motel, from which they have her conversation on tape, and know enough, is then she decides that it is in her best interest to make this work for her. 'If I give you any information, what's in it for me?'

'A lighter sentence, with early release,' says Fields.

'Well, you have almost everything that you need on tape, so what else do you want from me?' Jenny asks.

The conversation leads to Jenny and the officers devising a plan that Jenny will set up a meeting with Michael, in the hope that he can make a mistake. Sadly though, their efforts are all for nothing, because even though the meeting went as planned, it did not produce any further information.

The next step is to make a call to the local Judge to ask for a search warrant to inspect the property of a Michael Hubert of 36 Sundowner Avenue, Lidcombe. All the evidence is required for the judge to approve this, and three days later, it was all systems GO! Meanwhile, a team had to be assembled and a time had to be established. The evidence itself was not great, enough though for the warrant to be approved, but they needed more than a few timelines, and were still waiting on DNA results from the cigarette butts found at a few of the crime scenes. It was agreed upon by all team members of the Strike Force to have absolutely no communication with the suspect at all until they reached his house to execute the search warrant.

27

THE EVIDENCE

Early Wednesday morning, shortly after 6:30 a.m., and before Michael had a chance to leave for work, four squad cars quietly enter Sundowner Avenue, with eight officers in total. They arrive quietly, parking their cars on the driveway and on the road surrounding the home. A heavy banging on the door startles Louise and she drops her cup of tea, the cup smashing on the kitchen floor tiles. Michael is upstairs getting ready for work and hears the banging on the front door, instantly knowing that it was the police. He has seen enough movies to know the sound of police knocking on someone's front door when they meant business.

He yells out to Louise that he is on his way downstairs and would get the door. Though Louise has heard him clearly, she intends to find out just who is intruding at this early hour of the day. Not caring about the shards left by the broken tea cup or the spilt tea on the floor, she tightens her bath robe and makes her way to the front door. They both get to the front door at the same time, and Michael asks who is at the door.

'It's the police, Mr Hubert, we have a warrant to search your house. Please open the door.'

Both looked at each other in total disbelief and confusion.

'What is the warrant for,' pleads Michael.

'Just open the door and we can discuss this,' explains an officer.

Again, both look at each other with a questioning look and Michael slowly opens the door. Upon opening the screen door, an officer hands Michael the search warrant, but reading it makes no sense.

'What exactly are you looking for?' Michael asks.

'We are looking for further evidence in relation to the murders of a few recent bodies found that have a similar MO,' says Senior Constable Biggs.

He directs the officers to various parts of the house, while he and another officer inspect the garage. At first glance, it looks like an average garage. A long bench on one side with a number of drawers. A pegged board against the wall holding a variety of tools, including a hammer and screwdrivers. The hammer is taken into evidence. All the drawers are opened and sifted through, nothing looks suspicious. There is a fridge against the back wall, beside what looks like a bookshelf. The fridge is inspected and only beer and soft drink is found. SC Biggs starts to inspect the bookshelf, and firstly, does not notice anything out of the ordinary. He is about to walk away when he pushes against a shelf and the whole unit shifts. Feeling a breeze coming from underneath the bookshelf has raised suspicions.

'Hey, Richard, come and give me a hand with this,' says Biggs.

With a little effort, they are able to drag the shelving away from the wall, only to discover a hole behind it. A crawl space behind the wall, big enough for someone to comfortably walk into. The discovery is shocking. Inside are all kinds of things, a backpack, camera, jewellery, belts, among other things. Immediately the pressure is on, the mood goes into overdrive and SC Biggs quickly gathers a few more officers to bag and tag EVERYTHING in the crawl space.

He then finds Michael sitting on the lounge drinking coffee and approaches him.

'Please stand up, Mr Hubert, you are under arrest for the murders of two people. You have the right to remain silent. Anything you say, can, and will be used against you in the court of law. You have the right to speak to an attorney, and to have an attorney present during any questioning. If you cannot afford a lawyer, one will be provided for you at government's expense.'

Louise is stunned, shocked and in disbelief. 'What is going on here? You cannot take my husband. He hasn't done anything wrong. Michael, tell them you are innocent.'

Michael is just as shocked as his wife is and tells her that he'll sort it all out at the police station and not to worry. While Michael is being taken to Strathfield Police Station, the remaining officers continue their tireless work of collecting evidence. Louise sits with her head hung low, and cries. A female officer tries to comfort Louise but refuses to answer any of her questions, simply stating that she doesn't have the information required to satisfactorily answer her.

The police have basically ransacked her home, made a complete mess of her tranquil safe place. The whole process took them over an hour and left the place looking like a cyclone had gone through the place. All Louise could think to do was to open a fresh bottle of wine, pick her favourite wine glass from the kitchen cabinet and sit out on the back outdoor chairs and drink, drink until the bottle was empty, and then go for another bottle. Meanwhile, Michelle has decided to finally come out of her room and join her mother outside. On her way, she grabs a beer out of her dad's garage fridge and gathers the courage to tell her mum all about the incident where her father killed the next door's dog and buried it in the garden. Louise calls Michelle a liar, refusing to believe that Michael is not at all capable of such atrocities. Michelle stands her ground and goes into more detail about her observations about her dad. They both discuss it in detail for several hours, and the more they did, the more it all made sense.

The police escort Michael into an interview room to interrogate him, much to their frustration. They have collected a number of items including a hammer. What they haven't given consideration to, are the tools in Michael's work truck. The items have been sent to forensics for testing and will come back inconclusive. Meanwhile, Michael is questioned for the next fourteen hours about a number of issues. What type of cigarettes he smokes, where he was when the body in Lithgow went missing, which route he took on his trip to Bateman's Bay and what does he remember about the fishing trip. All throughout the interrogation Michael keeps claiming memory loss and tries to remain calm. If he lost his temper, it would definitely not work in his favour. It would just give the cops more to work with, and that's exactly what he needs to avoid.

After fourteen hours of questioning and Michael not giving the police anything that can convict him, they have no choice but to let him go. An officer offers to drive him home which he gladly accepted. Upon arriving at home, at around 11:00 p.m., the house is all dark. The front door not locked. As the police are pulling away, leaving him to sort out the aftermath, he slowly pushes the front door open, at first quietly calling out to Louise. No answer. Louder again and still no answer. No lights are on, so to avoid bumping into any furniture, he switches on the lounge room light. He is completely shocked at just how much destruction there was after the police had left. Why hadn't Louise attempted to clean the house? She always took pride in the appearance of her home. Now, he begins to worry and slowly walks upstairs. With each second or third step, he would call out to his wife. The closer he got to their bedroom, he could hear her snoring. So, before going to her, he checks Danielle's room and finds that she is asleep sideways on her bed, fully clothed. Weird, but, ok. Louise was also fully clothed and sleeping in an odd angle. He went to whisper to her to try and wake her when he could smell the wine. He immediately understood what he was seeing, so he carefully picks up his pillow and goes downstairs to sleep on the lounge. Though sleep seems to take forever to come as he is reliving the whole day in his head. How unbelievably quick things had gone, from slow and happy recovery to disaster. Tomorrow was a new day and he would talk to Louise and sort this mess out.

28

FINALLY OVER

The arrest really threw Michael, as he was totally unaware of what it was all about. Sure, he'd read a story or two recently about a few murdered bodies found, and currently, there are no suspects. So, when he was at the police station being questioned, he was adamant that he is innocent. He was held overnight at the police station cells, awaiting his lawyer – the items found in his garage are damaging. This is why he was not being released. 'Hello, Michael, I never thought that we'd be sitting here like this,' says his lawyer, Anton Dowd, from Dowd and Associates.

'You're late,' replies Michael in an annoyed tone. 'I've been sitting here all day and nobody is talking to me. I keep telling these arsehole cops that I have no idea how that stuff got in my garage. Sure, I have memory loss but it is just not something I would do.' 'Yes, the evidence points to you being responsible for these deaths. It's my job to convince the courts that you are not guilty of these crimes,' says Anton.

'We'll play on the amnesia and also try the mental health card. After what you have been through, it only makes sense,' Anton says.

'Monday, you are being arraigned for the first court hearing to hear the plea of your case. After that, it could be awhile before you get to the sentencing stage. I will visit again soon, but for now I need to talk to your family as my first step,' says Anton. That night Michael asked if it's possible to have a shower, it's been nearly two days since he last washed. He was bought a hamburger and coke from a shop close by for his evening meal, then allowed to wash up. He soaked up the hot water, the incredible feeling of it cascading down his body was more refreshing than he had expected. As he was stepping over the ledge that stops the water getting out all over the floor, he slipped. Fell flat on his arse and bumped his head on the wall, making him see stars. 'Great, all I need is a thumping frigging headache,' he complains. Luckily, he's on his own in the cell, so he has nobody to annoy him with incessant chatter. With nothing to do, no TV to watch, no book to read, he calls it a night. But that night, he remembered everything. He tossed and turned in his sleep, filled with awful and atrocious memories. He cannot let on that he now knows exactly what happened and has to pretend that the memory loss is still there.

Monday morning arrives with a loud clanging of keys unlocking his cell door. The officer on duty had a huge weekend and is in no mood for any shenanigans. 'Hubert, get up on ya feet. Stand facing the wall with your legs spread and your hands behind ya head.'

Michael is also not in the mood. The last thing he wants to do is piss this grumpy prick off. So, obligingly stands as asked, and is then handcuffed before being led through two corridors and into the parking bay, shoved into the back of the bull wagon, and left there for about fifteen minutes. Hard to really know, since he isn't wearing his watch. It felt more like an hour.

Finally, they get moving and are headed to Downing Centre Courts. Of course, Michael has no idea where they are going, as yet again he is not being told anything. Shit, even when he asks that grumpy prick, he just gets death stares and is told to keep moving. Strangely, Michael finds all of this shuffling, from the police station to the courthouse quite amusing. While no one is around, he has a big smirk on his face. It's like the circus has come to town and he's the main feature. He's brought straight up to level three and brought in through a side door, straight to the docks. The courtroom is eerily quiet, except for some paper ruffling, and the occasion whisper between lawyers and court staff. Then, five minutes later the court officer says, 'All rise, Judge Derek Marshall presiding.' Once the judge is seated, he tells everyone to sit, mobile phones are to be on silent or switched off and no photography is allowed. The member for the DPP states her name as Kimberley Porter. She then goes on to present her current information on this case and concludes by asking that bail be refused due to the nature of these crimes. Anton then explains his side of the argument, stating the memory loss and poor mental health means that he is of no threat and bail should be allowed. Again, you could hear the pin drop, it's that quiet, when suddenly the judge replies, 'After reading the evidence before me and the severity of this case, bail is refused, and the next available date for the case is in two weeks' time.'

So, Michael is dragged off and taken to Silverwater Correctional Centre, where he will have to wait until he's due back in court. He is placed in medium security, and in with criminals of all kinds.

He has been seen walking the yards with a mean-spirited attitude, sometimes mumbling to himself. Word spreads quickly that he is suspected of being a serial killer and the inmates tend to stay clear of him. Only twice does Anton visit him, and both times he didn't feel confident about his future. The items found in his garage were too obvious not to be anything else than the belongings of his victims. There were only two items that had actual identification on them. One was a purse with a photo ID and the other belonged to Stephanie.

Michael was unlucky to have a cellmate who was in for armed robbery. Apparently, he had held up several petrol stations armed with a sawn-off shotgun. Violence was easy for this guy whose mood swings were unpredictable. One night, Michael copped a beating because he had asked the wrong question at the wrong time. Needless to say, Michael never said another word when he was in his cell or anywhere near the lunatic.

Michael was due to appear in court the coming Wednesday, and he was glad to see the end of that hellhole. The case was heard early in the morning and continued until the end of the day. Arguments were given and the defence was given, a lot of evidence was also presented in this ongoing case. At the end of the day, the judge adjourned the case and would return to hear it at 10:00 a.m. the following day. That night was a cold one. A couple of sandwiches and orange juice was all he was given while held up in the local police station cells. One blanket in a concrete cell with a steel basin and toilet. He slept poorly. The next morning, with a horrible headache and in a dark mood, he was again dragged to the docks waiting for the judge.

Once the judge settled in, and after taking another five minutes of reading the files, he asked the DPP and Anton if there was anything else they had to disclose. Both agreeing that they have presented all of their information, the judge then asked Michael to please stand. 'Michael, you have been accused of the murders of Stephanie Myers and Hannah Henderson. . . and . . ., but also it has been spoken of your memory loss due to a previous accident, and the mental anguish of losing your daughter, I feel that I have no choice but to sentence you to serve five years in a mental facility linked to the Parklea Correctional Centre with a minimum twelve months non-parole period.' He was locked away for a year and a lifetime, and to make matters worse, his wife left him. Moved out of the family home. With her daughter, she moved to Queensland to start a new life. Incarceration was no holiday or picnic – twice a week, Michael had to sit down with a counsellor and pretend that he still had no recollection of the crimes that he'd been convicted of. One thing in his favour though was that he spends his time in a one-bed room that has a mini kitchenette where he can make coffee or reheat food in the microwave oven. Anton made a surprise visit about eleven months into his incarceration. Apparently, he was due to appear before the parole board. The counsellor has written a great review of their meetings throughout the year, and it is suggested that he is not a threat to society. The parole hearing takes place four months later. He is released with the condition of a Community Corrections Order for the remainder of his sentence. He has to report to Strathfield Police Station once a week for two years, and will be doing volunteer work with the Salvation Army stores as required, for a period of twelve months. After Michael is released, he is driven back to his home. Sadly, it has been neglected and there are badly overgrown lawns and gardens. With the loss of his job and family, he is alone to start all over again. Thankfully, he owns the house, so he doesn't have to worry about finding money for rent. The prison system allowed him to apply for unemployment benefits under special circumstances. He also has a moderately good bank account, so the first thing he organises is to have a landscape gardener come in and clean up his property. The inside of the house had never been cleaned after the search warrant raid. It took him just over a week to get it back to a liveable state. The following few months were mundane, with the usual routine of checking in at the police station and working at the Salvos. It was only a matter of time before things were to change. He was working in Auburn one week, and after finishing up, he decided to go down the road to the pub to grab something to eat and hopefully see a local band playing.

Across the room, near the exit doors, sat a woman on her own. He recognised the face but wasn't even sure what he was seeing was right. Jenny hadn't even seen Michael in the pub so when he approached her, she didn't know who he was at first. He explained how they had met a couple of years ago at the Oasis motel. He gave her a minute or two, and then the look on her face said it all. She invited him to sit and talk, but first insisted on buying a round of drinks. Michael explained everything from their last interaction and what has been happening since then. From the raid to the court case, and his wife leaving him. They sat for the next three hours chatting, but murder? That might have to wait until the next catch up.